hounding
the
truth

deadly possessions • book one

MELANIE PICKERING

Cover designed by Covered Up Book Designs
Edited by Crossbones Editing

ISBN: 978-0-6452945-7-6 (ebook)
ISBN: 978-0-6452945-8-3 (paperback)

First Edition: Published in Australia, July 2025
www.melaniepickering.com

Prologue

Leaving the Past Behind

Emily Sloane extended the handle on her rolling suitcase and took one last, sweeping glance at her old college apartment. The room was bare now, stripped of the books, thrifted artwork, and secondhand furniture that had once made it feel like home. Apart from a few more red wine stains on the carpet, it looked much the same as it had on the day she moved in. A blank canvas, brimming with possibility.

Much like she had been herself.

She hesitated at the threshold, gripping the key in her palm. If someone had told her six years ago—when she was just a fresh-faced eighteen-year-old, eager to carve out a future as a curator—that she'd one day walk away from a nearly completed master's degree in art history and an internship at one of Seattle's most prestigious galleries, she would have laughed in their face. The idea of abandoning everything she had worked for was absurd.

And yet, here she was.

1

Not just leaving but stepping into the unknown. In a matter of hours, she would board a flight halfway across the world to start a job she never applied for, working for a man she'd only met three weeks ago.

Jared Bell.

Line-cutter. Late-night Jacuzzi enthusiast. And director of one of Sydney's most exclusive auction houses at the tender age of twenty-nine. The mere thought of him sparked a thrill deep inside her, though whether from excitement or nerves, she wasn't entirely sure.

Theirs had been a chance meeting. She had been on her way to a family Christmas celebration in Leavenworth; he had been overseeing a business proposal for his brother before leaving for London. They were strangers passing through the same small town, staying at the same quaint cottage inn, with no reason to cross paths—until they did. He had jumped the queue in front of her. She had fainted right in front of him.

Neither was what you'd call a meet-cute. But she couldn't begrudge waking up in the strong Australian's arms.

It had all been the nutcrackers' fault, of course—four vintage brass blackbirds that she'd picked up from the antique table at a neighboring Christmas tree farm. The moment her fingers touched them, the past had come rushing in. A wave of grief, betrayal, something broken and unresolved. The vision had hit hard, and everything had gone black.

Later, over drinks at a local bar, she told him everything. About the psychic visions she'd been experiencing for as long as she could remember. About how she could see the past of objects just by touching them—an ability she'd learned to keep to herself and sidelined as intuition. Because most people dismissed it. Her ex had mocked it. Yet Jared did neither of those things.

He'd seen it for what it was: a gift.

Then, he'd offered her the chance to use it in a way that was meaningful.

Together, they'd traced the nutcrackers to their rightful owners, helping to close a decades-old wound neither of them had expected to uncover.

And somewhere between that moment and a midnight dip in the inn's hot tub, he'd asked her to come to Australia.

Not for a job, but for a purpose.

A clean slate.

A new beginning.

Locking the door behind her, Emily adjusted the strap of her purse and wheeled her suitcase down the hall, pressing the call button for the elevator. The building was mostly empty because of the holidays, and she was grateful for the quiet. Goodbyes were hard, and although telling her parents had been easier than expected, the send-off from her best friend Isobel last night had left her with both a punishing headache and a bruise in her chest that wouldn't fade anytime soon.

She drew in a lungful of the crisp damp air, her breath clouding, as she wheeled her suitcase toward the waiting cab. The driver offered a polite nod as he took her luggage and stowed it in the trunk.

As the cab pulled away from the curb, she closed her eyes, not wanting to see the damp, crowded streets she'd grown to love. Instead, she dreamed of sunshine and beaches and red dirt baking under an endless sky.

Because for once, Emily Sloane was determined *not* to look at the past.

I

The Hound of Blackwood Vale

"The beast did not snarl, nor did it advance. It only watched, its crimson eyes glowing like embers in the dark. It had been waiting for me, and now, at last, I had arrived."

~ The Hound of Blackwood Vale

Sydney, Australia

In the darkened corner of a basement storeroom, half a world away from everything she knew, Emily Sloane sipped her third consecutive cup of black coffee and stared down a hellhound. At least, it was what she imagined a hellhound to look like, if she ever had the misfortune of meeting one.

Beneath the glow of an overhead spotlight, strange shifting shadows danced along the creature's contours, and the longer she stared at it, the more it seemed to be watching her back. If its eyes had any color at all, Emily would swear they'd glow as red as the devil's.

The cold stone floor sent a shiver up her spine as she shifted her weight, the thin soles of her ballet flats offering little protection against the chill that had settled over her since she first encountered the hellish beast. The air in the storeroom had thickened at her approach, the scent of aged bronze rising like a warning. Cold, bitter. Not just metallic—but sharper. Like blood.

Emily knew better than anyone that antiques guarded their stories fiercely. Even when they wanted to speak, they rarely did so all at once. Some whispered, some resisted, and others—like the bronze hellhound—radiated a presence that was almost sentient. And for someone with her abilities, that usually meant trouble.

Taking another sip of coffee, she crouched down before the statue, silently grateful for having chosen to wear her tailored yet comfortable trousers. She'd had no idea what her first day working for Jared Bell would entail, but she hadn't expected to be immersed in the strange and fascinating task of authenticating items from a local horror author's deceased estate—a task that sent shivers down her spine and piqued her interest in equal measure.

Only four days had passed since she'd left the rainy streets of Seattle, and despite still battling jetlag, the anticipation of what lay ahead propelled her forward. There was something grounding about being here—something solid beneath the disorientation of travel and the surreal turn her life had taken. The weight of history clung to the place, quiet but unmistakable. It was a far cry from the sleek gallery spaces she'd once imagined working in, but this felt more honest. More alive.

Located just streets from Sydney Cove, the old warehouse had once stored liquor brought in by ship, its foundations laid by convict labor during the early penal settlement. Every brick had been hewn by hand, the natural variations in color not only a feature of the local sandstone but stained with the blood of the men who'd shaped them.

She'd be lying if she said she wasn't eager to touch those walls—to uncover their hidden stories—but doing so would have to wait for another time. She couldn't risk another dizzy spell, especially without Jared there to catch her. Up until that moment she'd fainted, her visions had never overwhelmed her like that. It must have taken all four nutcrackers at once to push her over the edge—but in a strange way, she was grateful they had. If not for that collapse, Jared might never have seen what she could do. They might never have had that conversation. He might never have offered her the job that had brought her here. *And he might never have kissed her in that hot tub under the stars...*

But that had been three weeks ago. Twenty-one days, 8,830 miles away, and a shift so stark it was as if they had reset entirely.

Ever since her arrival, the easy warmth they'd built in that small rural Washington town was gone, replaced with careful distance. Now that Jared Bell was her boss, she had accepted things would be different. Understood their need for professional boundaries. But after weeks of late-night messages filled with teasing banter—things that had hinted at *something more*—she hadn't expected to be banished to the basement on her first day. And not just the basement—but sub-level *three*.

It was like he was trying not to cross a line, even though he had already crossed it once. Did he regret what had happened between them?

Emily shook her head. She needed to focus if she had any hope of convincing him—convincing them both—that he hadn't just made a colossal mistake in flying her all the way out here to work for his family's company.

Finishing the coffee, she rose and reached for her company-issued iPad. It was the latest model, impossibly thin, and wrapped in a sleek custom-made cover in the company's signature navy blue. The suede folio was smooth beneath her fingertips, the embossed logo catching the light—and with it, a fleeting impression of Sofia Lange, Jared's stunning executive assistant, assembling everything Emily would need for her first day: the tablet, the company lanyard, the security pass that was now clipped to her waistband.

She exhaled, staring down at her ID photo. Historical Specialist. It sounded far more official than Psychic Researcher, but the job was the same. The past, waiting to be uncovered.

And this statue—looming, watching—was steeped in it.

Emily opened a blank object dossier and began her appraisal with a general description before moving on to any notable features. First impressions were paramount—often paving the way for her visions.

The surface patina of the life-sized bronze hellhound was a deep brown-black, its base and inner folds streaked with green oxidation—evidence of age and exposure to the elements. The front paws and haunches bore mild abrasion, consistent with years of handling or environmental wear. Any internal support appeared intact.

She turned on the camera, snapping a few close-up pictures. Photographing an exhibit wasn't technically part of her assignment, but she had discovered that viewing an object through a lens often revealed subtle details she might otherwise miss.

And this time, it was no different.

Through the high-definition lens, the Hound seemed to shift, its blank eyes tracking her movement with an unnatural awareness. The spotlight caught the curve of its snarling mouth, lending the illusion of motion. Its sinewy frame pressed forward despite the statue's rigid stillness, caught somewhere between lifeless alloy and wanting to move.

What should have been a static figure instead pulsed with raw potential—neither wholly guardian nor wholly beast, but something in between. Watching. Waiting.

Still, Emily knew better than to chase meaning where none had yet surfaced. She'd long since learned the past didn't appreciate being forced to speak. It surfaced in its own time, in its own way—and far more clearly when no one else was telling her what to hear.

As was her way, she had only asked for the essentials. No curator's notes, no background context—just the objects and space to listen. Jared had mentioned that the Hound statue was the centerpiece of an upcoming auction, drawn from the estate of gothic horror writer Victor Barrow. While unfamiliar with his works, Barrow's series of Blackwood novels had allegedly haunted readers for generations. And with the fiftieth anniversary of his most famous book approaching, public fascination with his life—and his mysterious death—was surging anew.

Bell's Fine Auctions had timed the sale accordingly. Decades-old manuscripts and personal items, once held back, were now being released as part of a major legacy auction. By aligning the launch with renewed interest, they were maximizing the collection's value at precisely the right moment. And Emily's role was critical: to trace the history buried within his possessions and uncover the truths they held, regardless of whether that aligned with what was recorded.

And those truths began with the eponymous Hound of Blackwood Vale, Barrow's most iconic and enduring creation.

Setting the iPad aside, she placed her palms on either side of the Hound's head, ready to uncover whatever secrets it held. The bronze felt intensely cold, its chill seeping into her bones with a shock that made her breath catch. Above, the lighting pulsed three times, then went dark, plunging the row into deep shadow. Emily flinched at the abrupt change, her pulse hammering in her ears. Still, she kept her hands firmly on the beast, grounding herself even as her vision began to waver and twist, the edges of reality folding into something otherworldly.

She inhaled deeply and surrendered to the pull, allowing her clairtangent ability to open her mind's eye. Reaching beyond the now, she opened a door into the past.

Victor Barrow's writing room is a bleak, suffocating space, gray and gloomy in the faded light of an afternoon storm. He sits hunched at a battered desk, surrounded by the remnants of his once-prominent life. Every available surface is filled with towers of books and yellowed sheets of paper. At his elbow, a stack of his own paperbacks support a heavy glass ashtray overflowing with cigarettes that have been smoked down to the filter.

Rain lashes the windows relentlessly, as if Nature itself seeks entry, but Victor's focus remains elsewhere. Distant. Consumed. His shaky fingers grip a thick-barreled Montblanc, the nib scratching across the pages of a hand-bound notebook. His writing is frantic, almost desperate, as if keeping the pen moving is the only thing preventing him from running out of time.

A crack of thunder rattles the windowpanes, and Victor jerks violently, the pen in his hand tearing a jagged gash through the paper. His breath quickens, and he glances over his shoulder, as if expecting someone—or something—to emerge from the shadows. But his gaze snags on the shelf by the door. Perched beside a row of books is a tarnished silver frame—inside, the face of his beloved Flo. For a fleeting moment, the sight of her soothes the ache in his chest, but the comfort is short-lived.

Outside in the darkness, the beast waits. Biding its time, patient and unyielding, watching as his body grows weaker with every passing hour. A crack of lightning splits the sky, and Victor's gaze snaps to the window, eyes wide and haunted with fear.

Reluctantly, he sets the pen down and buries his head in trembling hands. It's too late. He knows the truth. The hound he created, that snarling harbinger of doom, is more than mere fiction. It has become his undoing.

Death is coming for him, and on its heels is the snapping, hellish beast that will deliver him from this mortal life.

The sudden light struck Emily like a blow—too bright, too white. Searing, immediate. Her eyes, too used to the dark, couldn't adjust fast enough. Caught between her vision and the present, she flinched, stumbled, heart skipping as the shadows burned away.

"Hey, Em. You still down here?"

Jared's smooth voice, accompanied by the steady rhythm of his approaching footsteps, grounded her in the moment. Trying to make sense of what she'd just witnessed, she turned toward the familiar sound of him and promptly collided with his chest.

Concern etched his features as his hands gently grasped her elbows. "Are you okay?"

She felt him guiding her toward a velvet bench seat in the next row but Emily didn't want to sit. With her psychic channel still open, she'd prefer to avoid the lingering energy of anyone who'd rested upon that chair. More than that, just like the time she'd fainted, she wanted to be cocooned in his arms.

Disappointed, she pulled her hands from his. "I'm okay," she said with more reassurance than she felt. "I just need a moment to ground myself."

Heavy static clung to her skin like a sheen of sweat, as if the suffocating dread experienced by Victor Barrow had somehow seeped out of her vision and into her recovery. She shook out her limbs, brushed her bare skin, but the cobwebby feeling remained.

Jared fetched the bottle of water she'd left discarded with her things, handing it to her. "Here, drink this."

She took it from him gratefully and took a few cooling sips. "At least I stayed standing this time."

"That bad, huh?" He tilted his head, assessing her with patience and quiet concern.

"Bad enough."

He cleared his throat, gaze dipping to her lips, causing her pulse to quicken. "I haven't had breakfast yet. How about we go upstairs, grab some fresh air, and you can tell me all about it over omelets?"

She supposed that three cups of espresso on an empty stomach probably wasn't the best remedy for her remaining jetlag, and might explain the jittery edge she was still feeling. He waited while she gathered her things, and together, they crossed the floor toward the elevator.

As they waited for the lift, Emily glanced back down the aisle to where Victor Barrow's collection was stored. The light above the shelving flickered again, then blinked out. *Motion-activated*, she reminded herself. But something about it needled her.

The bulb had dimmed the instant she touched the Hound, or so she'd thought. And it hadn't come back on—not until Jared had approached.

Her stomach tightened. She'd been standing there longer than she thought—silent, unmoving, like a statue herself in the dark.

Her visions usually struck like lightning: brief, disorienting flashes of the past that vanished almost as soon as they came. But this one had *lingered*—drawn out and uncomfortably vivid, as if she'd stepped straight into someone else's nightmare and forgotten how to find her way out. She'd never even heard of Victor Barrow before today. Now, his ghost was everywhere.

Could he truly have been haunted by the beast he created? Or had the lines between fiction and reality merely blurred for him in the end?

Whatever the truth, Emily was determined to find it.

2

A History of Fear

*"The villagers did not speak of the Hound
unless pressed, and even then, their voices
fell to whispers, their eyes darting to the
shadows, as if the mere mention of it might
summon its wrath."*

~ The Blight on Blackwood Heath

Jared's suggestion of breakfast was both unexpected and welcome. Emily hadn't realized just how tightly she'd been holding herself until the sunlight hit her skin, the tang of briny seawater fresh in the air. They'd found a quiet table on the patio of a harborside cafe tucked just far enough away from the tourist bustle. The only sounds were the waves slapping against the pier and seagulls squabbling on the sidewalk.

She dug into a golden omelet folded over bacon and mushrooms, grateful for the grounding simplicity of it. Across from her, Jared stirred sugar into his coffee, waiting—not pushing—for her to speak.

It took her until she was halfway finished to tell him. About Victor. The storm. The frenzied writing and the fear that didn't belong to the present.

All the while, Jared listened, eyes fixed on her, his expression unreadable until the last detail left her lips. Then his brow furrowed. "Are you absolutely sure you've never read anything by Victor Barrow?" he asked carefully.

Emily blinked. "I'd never even heard of him until this morning. Why?"

"Because what you described... it could've been lifted straight out of one of his novels."

She sat back, fork idle on her plate. "Wait—are you saying I made it up?"

"No." His voice, while apologetic, was firm. "I'm saying it sounds like you *tapped into* something." He reached forward, his gaze intense. "You know I trust in your ability. In you."

Her eyes dropped to his open palm. It wasn't just the words he spoke—it was the way he said them. Like he'd never questioned her gift, even when she still did sometimes. It was why she hadn't written him off that first day, despite the effortless charm and the wicked smile that belonged to someone far too used to getting his way.

She placed her hand in his big warm one. "Okay, so what do I do now?"

"I think it's time I introduced you to my rare books specialist," he said, pulling her to her feet.

Whether it was her now-full belly, or the comforting knowledge that she hadn't screwed up her first morning on the job, exhaustion set in. She was almost over the jetlag, but she was going to need more caffeine to get through the day.

"I'm just going to grab another coffee to go."

Jared hesitated. "I don't know if that's a good idea, Em."

"Okay. Right. Bad idea. Probably. But maybe an iced latte? That's basically milk with... barely even coffee. Enough to trick my brain into functioning without totally wrecking what's left of my sleep cycle. Or my dignity."

It was probably too late for that, but she didn't care. "Sorry, that was a lot. I'm tired."

He blinked at her, bemused. "Okay. One iced latte coming up."

"On oat milk, please."

He failed to hide his grimace. "You know we have cows in Australia, right?"

She laughed as he headed for the counter, appreciating the way his shirt stretched across the breadth of his shoulders and outlined his biceps. His sleeves, casually pushed to the elbows like half the men she'd seen that morning, revealed taut, tanned muscle, his gold-banded smartwatch catching the sunlight as he tapped it for payment.

Whether it was just the summer heat or the laid-back Aussie way, Emily had noticed male business attire here was much more... forgiving than back in Seattle. Jackets were slung over chairs, ties forgotten, top buttons undone, and forearms of every kind—tanned, inked, freckled, flexed—were on unapologetic display.

Isobel would be feral.

Her best friend had a well-documented appreciation for arm-candy—especially the kind that came with rolled cuffs and vascular definition. Emily almost reached for her phone, ready to snap a pic of the cafe crowd with a witty caption like: *Whose arm is it anyway?*

But Jared turned just then, with two lattes in hand, and she quickly slid her phone back into her purse.

Still, she felt the ache of distance in that moment, of wanting her best friend's voice in her ear—quick witted and irreverent—making wildly inappropriate guesses about which forearm belonged to her hot boss and ranking them all by dateability.

Emily had all but finished her latte by the time they reached the auction house, and Jared ushered her inside, taking the lift up to the second level. There, he introduced her to a smiling middle-aged man with curling brown hair and twinkling eyes.

"Emily, this is Michael Winslow. If there's anything about Victor Barrow that Mike doesn't know, it won't exist." Jared winked as he left, his fingers brushing her lower back in a way that went far beyond simple reassurance.

Turning to hide the blush that no doubt stained her cheeks, Emily glanced around the rare books room, expecting grand timber bookshelves and the comforting scent of aging paper and warm leather bindings. Instead, the climate-controlled air was sterile and dry, laced with only the faintest earthy undertone. Goosebumps prickled her bare arms, a chill intensified by the icy coffee she'd gulped down, and she instantly regretted not having stopped by her office for her blazer first.

"I hear you're looking for an introduction to the world of *Blackwood*," Michael said, appearing with a navy anorak embroidered with Bell's insignia.

Emily offered a grateful smile as she slipped it over her shoulders. "Total newbie, I'm afraid."

He grinned. "Then let's see what we can do about that."

Emily warmed to the man immediately. He reminded her of a favorite uncle back home in the States, with his checked oxford and vintage brown corduroy jacket. Unlike her Uncle Pete, however, Michael moved swiftly and with purpose, directing her to sit in a leather chesterfield while he busied himself pulling several books down from one of the many glass-fronted cabinets that lined the room.

"Ah, here we are."

Emily took a pair of nitrile gloves from a box beside the lounge and pulled them on as she surveyed the lurid covers spread out across the coffee table. Designed to hook eyeballs and thrill readers, the covers of the *Blackwood* series featured dark, foreboding landscapes—either thickly wooded forests or moonlit moorlands—each with the smudged black silhouette of the Hound lurking in the foreground. She realized with some satisfaction that the creature's eyes were indeed depicted as diabolically red, just as she had imagined.

The books themselves were classic pulp: pocket-sized paperbacks typical of the late seventies and early eighties—mass-produced for distribution into bookstores, airports, and the like. But the copies in front of her didn't have the faded, tattered covers and foxed pages like those found among the cramped shelves of any bargain-basement secondhand bookstore. No, these were pristine first editions, signed by Victor Barrow himself.

Careful not to crack the spines, Emily's eyes widened as she recognized the faded blue-black ink from her vision—the same ink she was certain had come from the Montblanc fountain pen Barrow had used to feverishly scrawl what she now knew were his final words. The back of her neck prickled at the memory of his haunted expression and the palpable scent of fear that had permeated the room.

"So, Barrow only wrote five books in his career?" she asked.

"That was considered quite prolific for the time," Michael replied. "Most horror writers in the eighties stuck to stand-alone novels, but the *Blackwood* series was different. Although each book could be read independently, they were interconnected in ways that were unique back then." He took the seat across from her, removing his glasses and setting them aside. "Barrow published a book every three years like clockwork and amassed a cult-like following. The series began with *The Hound of Blackwood Vale* in 1978. Then came *The Ghosts of Blackwood Ridge*, *The Blight on Blackwood Heath*, *The Curse of Blackwood Bay* and ended with *The Haunting of Blackwood Manor* in

1990. Pendleton Press, his long-time publisher, even hinted that he was working on a sixth book before his death in '93, but of course no manuscript has ever surfaced."

Emily's mind flashed back to her vision. Had Barrow been desperately trying to finish that elusive sixth book, knowing something sinister was closing in on him?

"How exactly did he die?" she asked, her voice barely above a whisper.

Michael leaned forward, a glimmer of intrigue in his eyes. "Well, that's the real mystery, isn't it?"

Emily leaned forward, too. "I don't follow."

"You see, the official cause of death was a heart attack at his desk," Michael said. "But according to the rumors, Barrow was found outside in his garden, drenched from an overnight storm, and slumped over the statue of The Hound of Blackwood Vale."

"You mean the one downstairs?"

"The very same."

Emily pondered that for a moment. "And what do *you* think happened?"

Michael's lips curled into a knowing smile. "Much like his novels, Victor Barrow was an enigma. He arrived here in Sydney from England in the seventies, with no family to speak of and a dark imagination that captured a nation of readers. He brought an entirely British mythical creature, the Black Shuck, with him into the Australian landscape and the population ate it up. You'll hear that the beast boarded a convict ship bound for

Van Diemen's Land, or that Barrow was inspired while staying with friends along the bleak coastal heathlands of north-western Tasmania. Many have searched the area far and wide, hoping to glimpse the infamous black hellhound for themselves, but no one has ever laid claim to have found it. It's isolated, harsh country. No one could survive out there for too long."

Emily shuddered. *Especially if there was a monstrous black dog on the loose.*

"But that doesn't really answer your question, does it?" Michael gave a small, wistful smile. "What I'm trying to say is that Barrow was an eccentric recluse with a flair for the macabre, and he knew exactly how to keep people guessing. He was notoriously tight-lipped about his inspiration, which only fueled the rumors. He would have relished the intrigue and the hype his work still stirs up after all these years."

So, Barrow clearly had friends and obviously a wife or lover whose photo he kept on his bookshelf. Who was his "beloved Flo"? And what had become of her?

"You said that Barrow arrived without family. But did he ever marry, or have children?" she prompted.

"He took a wife, Florence Rushby, whom he met here in Sydney, and the couple settled in Vaucluse." Here, Michael paused, his expression softening. "Sadly, she died some ten years before him, and they weren't blessed with any children. Still, until her death, she remained Victor's greatest fan. Did you know it was Florence who commissioned the statue to celebrate the publication of *The Hound of Blackwood Vale*? She even had it installed in the garden of their manor, where he could view it from his writing room."

Emily's fingers gripped the arm of the lounge as her ears rang with a sudden rush of blood. Never mind that her vision had confirmed Victor's wife; her heart was pounding with the revelation of what Barrow had been staring at that night.

It was the Hound. He'd been watching it through the window all along.

The rest of Emily's first day at Bell's passed in a blur. After spending hours immersed in the gothic horror of Victor Barrow, she finally retreated to her new office to finish her report on the statue and the other items belonging to the late author. His vintage Remington typewriter had given her nothing, despite her hope that it might somehow echo the words from his lost manuscript. But she knew from her vision that he'd preferred to write longhand, and neither his Montblanc pen nor the infamous sixth manuscript had ever surfaced during the initial acquisition. Still, cataloging the collection had been thrilling, if not exhausting.

To celebrate making it through the day, Jared insisted on taking the entire team out for dinner, and Emily welcomed the chance to unwind. Her head was still swimming with details of Barrow's life, and despite keeping the morning's weariness at bay, she was bone tired.

They met in the lobby, where Sofia was coolly negotiating a last-minute table at one of the city's most exclusive restaurants. Jared strode up and plucked the phone from her fingers without missing a beat.

"Nope," he said. "Emily's initiation calls for something authentically Australian. Pub, not prix fixe."

Sofia looked momentarily affronted—then let out a long-suffering sigh, murmuring something in Swedish that Emily suspected wasn't entirely flattering.

Still, Emily offered a smile. Sofia was all precision and silent competence—Jared's laconic style must drive her mad. She'd first met his personal assistant on arrival in Sydney, when Sofia collected her from the private terminal after midnight, navigated her through immigration like a seasoned diplomat, and then delivered her to Jared's front door with suitcase in hand and not a hair out of place.

Emily had liked her immediately.

Jared waited until everyone was gathered, before ushering the group outside and down the street to a lively hotel nestled just a short walk away in the historic precinct known as The Rocks.

The balmy evening air and the relaxed atmosphere were exactly what Emily needed to clear away the cobwebs of the day's strange events and push through the last of her jetlag. Once they'd all found a place to sit at a long outdoor table and had a cold drink in hand, Jared stood up, clearing his throat loudly. Emily looked up to find him gazing down at her with twinkling eyes. He laid a hand on her shoulder, the warmth of his fingers seeping through the thin silk of her strappy blouse. When his thumb began tracing small circles on her bare shoulder in a silent acknowledgment of the connection between them, she almost melted under his touch.

"I'd like to take a moment to officially welcome Emily Sloane into the Bell's family," he said, lifting his glass with a warm smile. "I know your introduction has been a bit of a whirlwind, but these amazing people are here to support you every step of the way. So, don't hesitate to lean on them when you need it—whether it's help with an appraisal, figuring out the office coffee machine, or even just a chat after a long day."

"Don't bother with the coffee machine, it's crap," Sofia murmured, and everyone laughed.

Jared regarded the group with genuine affection. "We're thrilled to have you on board, Emily. Here's to new beginnings, new friends, and making incredible things happen together."

Unwavering, his gaze burned into her even as the table erupted with cheerful clinking glasses and welcoming shouts. Emily blushed furiously, not used to being the center of attention. She never imagined mixing business with pleasure like this—alfresco dining on a cobblestone street with her colleagues and her irresistibly charming boss.

She looked away from the heat in his eyes as he sat beside her with a playful smile.

"I hope you're not having second thoughts."

"Not at all," she said, her gaze drifting toward the glowing

26

lanterns. "Just thinking how different my Monday nights used to be."

He leaned in slightly. "Such as?"

"Back home it was red wine, greasy burgers, and yelling at the TV with Isobel during Monday Night Football. She's a diehard Seahawks fan—I only tuned in for the Huskies. We'd argue over popcorn toppings more than the score." Her smile turned wistful. "I miss her."

Jared nudged her gently with his shoulder. "Well, we've got football here, too. It just looks different. You can pick a team, barrack with the rest of us, and I'll make sure the kitchen stocks red wine and popcorn."

She laughed, the tension in her chest easing just a little. But before the moment could stretch too far or settle too deeply, a booming voice with a sharp Scottish burr cut through the hum of conversation.

"Oi, Jared! Word is Pendleton Press are keen to get their mitts on the Barrow collection."

The publisher's name drew Emily's attention, and she twisted in her seat to face Gareth Macalister, Bell's senior auctioneer. He was late-thirties, younger than she had expected given his title, though the flecks of gray threading through his dark hair and beard hinted at a career long enough to earn it. His presence carried an easy authority, and all eyes turned his way, as well.

Michael had hinted earlier that Pendleton was eager to get their hands on Barrow's elusive final manuscript, but since that wasn't part of Bell's inventory, Emily couldn't figure out what they would hope to gain at the auction.

"Wouldn't they already have his manuscripts?" she asked out loud.

"They would, for sure," Jared said, leaning closer. "But they're keen to collect everything."

"So it is true, then," Gareth replied, a sly, wolfish grin splitting his face.

"And guess who else is sniffing around?" added a middle-aged woman seated across from Emily. "Barrow's ghostwriter."

"Barrow didn't have a ghostwriter," Michael cut in. "Simon Reed's involvement was never more than a rumor, Carmel."

"Rumors have value, though," Jared mused, his gaze shifting thoughtfully to the woman. Carmel, presumably, turned her sharp chocolate brown gaze on Michael with barely disguised triumph.

"What does Reed want?" Jared asked.

"The Hound," she said. "And he's demanding an early inspection."

Gareth scoffed loudly. "As if that'll ever happen."

Emily's attention bounced from one face to another as everyone at the table weighed in, each with their own theory or piece of inside knowledge. The air buzzed with a mixture of excitement and speculation, all centered on the Hound of Blackwood Vale. Personally, she didn't understand the appeal. The sculpture might be a work of art, but it was also incredibly eerie. Not something she'd like to have in her house, *or garden*, she thought with a shudder.

After a couple of hours, the rest of the team congratulated Emily on her first day before heading off, leaving her and Jared alone. He'd graciously offered her the guest room in his two-bedroom loft on the top floor of the auction house until she found a place of her own, and as he walked her back, the night air grew heavy with the promise of rain. Storm clouds had been gathering out over the harbor all evening, their dark bellies flickering with lightning.

Inside, it was cool despite the humidity of the creeping storm, the ducted air conditioning humming quietly. Jared's space was layered with rich textures and understated luxury—Persian rugs scattered across hardwood floors, an eclectic mix of antique furniture arranged with effortless ease. The vaulted ceiling, stark white against thick timber beams, gave the loft an airy feel, countered by a rugged masculinity that was undeniably his.

"Champagne?" he offered, already reaching inside the fridge for a bottle.

Emily dropped her purse onto the sofa and sank into the plush cushions with a laugh. "Haven't we done enough celebrating?"

"This is a personal congratulation," he said, popping the cork on a bottle of Moet and pouring them each a glass. "I couldn't be happier that you decided to join me, Em. But how are you feeling about everything?"

"Tired, but in a good way."

"I promise not to work you too hard tomorrow," he teased,

taking a seat beside her.

She gave him a playful smile. "Are you kidding? I'd expect nothing less."

They chatted for a bit, but it had been a long day and Emily couldn't suppress another yawn. Jared noticed immediately, setting down his glass and standing.

"Alright, time to get you to bed."

He offered his hand, and she let him pull her to her feet, falling into step behind him as he led the way to the guest room. Since her arrival, Jared had been giving her space, staying at his parents' home so she could adjust to the move and sleep off her jetlag in a place that felt both safe and familiar. The thoughtful gesture hadn't gone unnoticed, but it also made it impossible to forget that he was treating her as more than just an employee.

"Thanks again for letting me stay here," she said as they reached the door. "I'll start looking for an apartment tomorrow."

"You're welcome to stay as long as you want," he replied, his voice dropping to a low murmur that hinted at something she really shouldn't hope for. A few weeks of flirty texts since that kiss hadn't exactly established them as a couple, but the pull between them was undeniable. And if the way his gaze held hers now was a sign, it was obvious he felt it, too.

Thunder rumbled outside, and Emily glanced toward his bedroom. "You should stay here tonight. With that storm coming and all."

For a moment, Jared seemed to weigh her words, a flicker of

something unreadable crossing his face. Then he nodded, his eyes lingering on her mouth. "Okay. I'll be just down the hall if you need me. Sleep well, Em."

He pressed a kiss to her forehead before they bade each other goodnight. Emily closed her door and leaned against it, listening to him tidy up but wishing he were standing on the other side, feeling the same way she was. Beyond her window, the sky continued to flicker with lightning; the storm biding its time. Even with the central cooling, the air inside her room felt oppressive, charged, like the night itself was holding its breath. Or maybe that was just her.

Closing the drapes, she undressed and slipped between the sheets. Her body was heavy with exhaustion, yet her thoughts refused to settle. Her mind swirled with unanswered questions about the auction and the revelations uncovered tonight regarding Pendleton and Simon Reed.

And then there was Jared's offer, and the knowledge that he was spending the night just down the hall—his solemn assurance that he'd be there if she needed him. But how far exactly did he intend to take that promise?

Emily sighed and closed her eyes, but sleep, it seemed, would remain maddeningly out of reach.

3

Visions and Nightmares

"The scratching at my door had become a nightly ritual, a doomed promise in the dead hours. Whatever lingered beyond the threshold was patient. And patience, I feared, was far more dangerous than hunger."

~ The Ghosts of Blackwood Ridge

The storm arrives with a vengeance, shaking the very bones of the house with each thunderous boom. My eyes snap open, my breath sharp and uneven. Lightning streaks across the ceiling, casting jagged, shifting shadows that crawl across the walls like grasping fingers.

Something is wrong.

Rising from the bed, I cross the floor, a heavy sense of dread pressing down on me, thick and choking like smoke. My fingers brush the cool glass of the windowpane before settling on the knob of a set of French doors—doors I'm certain weren't there before.

A chill prickles along my spine.

My hand trembles as I twist the knob, the wind roaring through the widening gap, tearing the door from my grasp. It slams against the outer wall with a deafening crack, the sound swallowed by the storm's fury. Rain lashes at my skin, plastering my chemise to my body as my hair whips across my face, blinding me.

I stagger back, confusion clawing at the edges of my mind. This isn't Jared's loft.

The sharp tang of petrichor fills the air, but something else taints it—the rank, cloying scent of rotting leaves... and dampened fur.

A guttural growl rumbles through the night.

My heart stutters, my body rigid as the sound seems to come from everywhere and nowhere at once. But despite the primal fear sinking its claws into my chest, something compels me forward. Something is waiting for me. Something only I can face.

With my bare feet sinking into the sodden earth, I push deeper into the darkened garden, breath hitching as the twisted branches of a massive weeping fig stretch toward me like skeletal hands. Lightning arcs overhead, and in the brief flash of brilliance, I see it—The Hound.

Barrow's Hound.

I must reach it before it's too late.

A root snares my foot, and my ankle twists, sending me sprawling onto the wet dirt. Pain lances through my knees. Brushing mud and leaf litter from my hands, I scramble to my feet, staggering toward the statue, hands outstretched. I reach the slick marble pedestal and scramble up it, my hands around the Hound's neck, rainwater sluicing from the beast's open muzzle into my eyes.

Lightning flares again, and the Hound is gone.

My breath catches. Falters.

I curl up on the marble block as a coughing spasm takes hold, shadows pooling and shifting around me, gathering into something vast and blacker than the night itself. A suffocating sense of dread presses down on my chest, a dark and malevolent presence that's somehow both familiar and menacing.

Then—

A pair of crimson eyes flare to life in the darkness, smoldering red, ancient and unrelenting.

A scream lodges in my throat as the weight of the presence bears down on me, crushing, inescapable...

Emily sat up in bed, drenched in sweat and gasping for breath. Her bedroom door burst open, and Jared filled the doorway, bare-chested and wide-eyed.

"Em!" he shouted over the rumble of thunder, moving to her bedside. "Are you all right?"

"I..." She looked around the room as the smell of wet dog

intensified. "Yeah, I'm okay. Just a bad dream, I think." She reached for the bottled water beside her with shaking hands and drank it dry. "Sorry if I woke you."

He sank down beside her on the bed, raking a hand through his golden hair, leaving it irresistibly tousled. "You screamed pretty loud. It sure gave us a fright."

"Us?" Emily blinked at him, confused.

His smile was soft, almost apologetic, as he turned toward the door. "Lucy, it's okay. You can come in."

Lucy? Emily's stomach clenched at the name, her pulse quickening with an irrational stab of jealousy. *He has another woman here?* Her chest tightened with an ache she had no right to feel.

Aware that she was practically naked beneath the sheets, Emily opened her mouth to protest, but her breath hitched as a dark muzzle and a pair of glittering eyes emerged from the shadows.

"Come on, Luce." Jared patted the bed, his tone light with encouragement.

Emily's chest tightened for a completely different reason as a massive black dog padded silently into the room, pointed ears flicking forward like a radar. It sat obediently at Jared's feet, eyes locked onto her with unwavering focus.

"This is Lucy," Jared explained, scratching the dog's head affectionately. "She's my mom's pup. Lucy, meet Emily."

"Pup?" Emily echoed faintly, her throat dry. She couldn't tear her eyes from the large canine. The oppressive weight of her dream—the storm, the Hound, the chase—all came rushing back in a suffocating wave. Her fingers tightened in the bedsheets as she took in Lucy's short, jet-black coat and the ridge of thick fur running like a razor's edge down her back.

There was no mistaking the source of the wet dog smell now. And there was no mistaking the sharp intelligence in Lucy's dark eyes as she crept forward, her movements deliberate and predatory.

Jared laughed, his warm voice breaking the tension. "She's hoping you have treats," he said, ruffling Lucy's ears as though the animal hadn't just sent a chill down Emily's spine.

She forced a smile, though her pulse thundered in her ears. The room suddenly felt too small, too still. She swallowed hard and tried to steady her breathing.

It wasn't that Emily was afraid of dogs. In fact, she and her ex had spoken of getting one when they got married, and Alex had known someone who bred some sort of "Oodle"—one of those designer mixed breeds that didn't shed. Personally, Emily would have preferred to rescue a shelter dog, but she hadn't pushed the issue. If compromising with Alex meant they could have a fur baby, she figured it was a small price to pay. Of course, they'd never settled down, and therefore, she had little experience with canines. Especially ones of this size.

"Uh, hello, Lucy. What are you doing here?" she asked.

At the sound of her name, the dog tilted her head, her sharp ears twitching. A soft whine escaped her muzzle as she shuffled closer, her wet nose brushing Emily's thigh through the sheet.

"She looks dangerous, but won't hurt you," Jared said with a reassuring smile. "Poor Luce hates storms, and with Mom and Dad away in Portugal, I didn't want to leave her home alone tonight, so I drove over to grab her. Good thing I did—she was completely drenched by the time I got there. Weren't you, girl?"

Emily extended her hand for Lucy to sniff and was rewarded with a tentative lick.

"See, she likes you," Jared said with a grin so broad he looked almost boyish. Of course, there was nothing boyish about the half-naked man sitting on her bed. Especially when he lifted those piercing blue eyes to hers. "Feeling better?"

Emily swallowed. *Was she?* To be honest, she wasn't entirely sure. The nightmare had already left her shaken, a lingering unease twisting in her gut—and then Lucy had appeared, like a page torn straight out of one of Barrow's novels. Had Lucy somehow influenced her dream, or was it the other way around?

Deep down, Emily couldn't shake the feeling that Lucy's sudden presence was far more than coincidence.

"Has this sort of thing happened before?" Jared asked once they had settled in his living room with a pot of calming herbal tea.

She lifted a shoulder. "Sort of. I mean, everyone has nightmares, right? Probably just too much alcohol and horror stories before bed."

It had only been a dream—she told herself that—but dreams had never bled into her visions before. And never like that—slipping through sleep, stealing her breath, leaving her heart hammering long after she woke.

Jared shook his head, his stubbled jaw tightening as he looked away. At his feet, Lucy looked up at him and whined. "No, this is all on me. I shouldn't have thrown you into something so heavy straight away. I didn't think about how Barrow's words would affect you. And I should have. I should have realized that you'd naturally tap into what he was feeling as he wrote." He rubbed the back of his neck, clearly struggling with guilt. "Knowing how dark his work is—"

"Hey." Emily reached across the arm of the sofa and took his hand in her own. "It's not your fault, Jay. This is all part of the job."

He glanced down at her hand, then to her face, concern still darkening his eyes. "Doesn't matter. I should've eased you in. Picked a different collection."

"Absolutely not. This is exactly why you hired me." She held his gaze, her voice steady. "Don't treat me differently, Jared. Please. I mean it."

He hesitated, then brought her fingers to his chest. "Are you sure that's what you want, Em? Because I don't usually comfort employees in the middle of the night." He leaned closer, his gaze dipping briefly to where her robe was parted. "Especially when they're wearing nothing but a slip of satin."

Heat flooded her cheeks. Obviously, his treating her like just an employee wasn't what she wanted. But it *should* be.

"I didn't think so," he murmured, a faint smile tugging at his lips as if he knew exactly what she was thinking.

He was still dressed in nothing but the sleep shorts he'd been wearing earlier, which she wasn't so sure he'd even slept in, and she let herself admire his swimmer's build—narrow hips, broad shoulders, all understated strength. The sight reminded her of the first night she'd seen him, or rather, ogled him. When they had both stayed at the same cottage inn outside Leavenworth, and he'd shown up in the middle of the night, making a tremendous racket before settling into the hot tub just outside her room. She really couldn't have not looked. At least that's what she kept telling herself.

"You know," she said, glancing at him with a faint smirk, "I never would've pegged you as the type to cure insomnia with tea. I figured Jacuzzis were more your style."

He flashed a small grin. "That's Mom's British genes for sure, plus I spent a few years in London. And as for Jacuzzis, I haven't exactly felt inclined to step into one since... well, somehow, it's just not the same without you." Leaning back into the armchair beside her, he stretched out with easy confidence, one ankle propped on the opposite knee, his bronzed chest and toned shoulders still on display.

She squeezed her thighs together, the memory of that night unspooling in her mind like something forbidden. "You know, you could put a shirt on or something," she said, her tone light but betraying her flustered state.

Jared's brow lifted, amusement dancing in his eyes. "You've seen me in less, Em."

Her cheeks burned as that starry night surged forward—just the two of them cocooned in the steaming water, a little tipsy on holiday cheer and something far more intoxicating.

"Yes, I'm *well aware*," she murmured into her tea, not quite able to meet his gaze.

To her relief—and slight disappointment—Jared pushed himself up and strolled down the hall, returning moments later in a gray muscle shirt that covered his abs but did little to conceal the breadth of his shoulders or the bulge of his biceps.

She really needed to get her own place. Soon.

"So," she said, forcing boldness into her tone as she set her cup down. "Who's Simon Reed?"

Jared stooped to gather Lucy into his arms, lifting the big dog before settling her onto his lap. She huffed once, content, and rolled onto her back. Jared chuckled and began stroking his fingers slowly up and down her belly.

Then, softly—almost distractedly—he murmured, "Good girl."

Emily's breath caught. It was nothing, just a throwaway line to the dog. But the way his voice dipped when he said it—low, warm, threaded with authority—sparked heat deep in her core.

Lucy gave a happy grunt, oblivious. But Emily squirmed in her seat, trying not to imagine trading places with the dog. She crossed her legs and shifted her cup out of arm's reach, fingers suddenly unsteady.

"Are you sure you want to talk shop right now?" Jared asked her with a frown.

"I'm fine. Plus, it might help me make sense of the nightmare. I figure it must have been triggered by something I read today or overheard at dinner." She shrugged, the movement causing her robe to slip down over her bare shoulder.

Jared's gaze snagged on it and lingered. He cleared his throat. "Michael didn't fill you in today?"

"We only spoke about Barrow. And his wife."

"Well, Mike's the expert. I don't know much about Simon Reed other than he was pegged as a rising star in horror fiction during the '90s—or so the story goes. He was young, ambitious, but couldn't get a foot in the door with publishers. That's where the rumors start. Worried about Barrow's declining health and determined to keep the Blackwood series alive, Pendleton allegedly brought Reed on as a ghostwriter. But, as you know, the series came to an abrupt halt after the fifth book, anyway."

"So, Reed never published under Barrow's name?"

"Not that we're aware of. He either went underground after Victor's death or wrote under a pseudonym."

Emily pondered this new information while finishing her tea. "For a director, you seem to know an awful lot about this collection."

Jared chuckled. "Well, Mom was a curator for many years. It's second nature, but I make it my job to know as much as I can about what flows through those front doors. Not everything is about the bottom line. It's what sets us apart from the competition."

He'd told her as much back in December, on their way to Baltimore to return the blackbird nutcrackers to their former owners. "But why auction all this off now?" she asked him. "Won't it just look like you're capitalizing on Barrow's anniversary to make the most money?"

"As opposed to capitalizing on his death?" He raised a brow, and she bit her bottom lip. He made a fair point. Clearing Victor's estate right away would have been in poor taste. What did she know about running an auction house, anyway? She ought to stick to what she knew.

"Wait." She withdrew her legs from the couch and sat up as a possibility formed in her mind. "There's still rumored to be a missing manuscript, though, right?"

"I can see where you're going with this, but—"

"Hear me out, okay? What if Simon Reed actually wrote the sixth book, and he's had the manuscript all this time?"

Jared stared at her for a moment. "But wasn't Victor working on the manuscript in your vision?"

"That's what I thought at first. But to be honest, I didn't see what he was writing. I only assumed he was madly trying to finish a book, because that's what it looked like. But maybe it was just a journal, or a letter, or something totally non-related."

Jared ran his finger over his bottom lip in thought. "It would certainly explain Pendleton's interest in wanting to collect all the remaining manuscripts. Especially if they think Victor was stalling on approving Reed's draft."

"Right. Except we know that the sixth manuscript isn't in the lot. But it would explain Victor's paranoid behavior in my vision. Jared, what if Victor was penning the truth of what was happening between him and Simon Reed?"

"You think Barrow knew he was being edged out of the series and Reed killed him to hasten the plan?"

"What I think"—Emily stood and fixed her robe—"is that I need to get inside Barrow's estate."

4

Tea at the Manor

"Bitter leaves swirled in the cup's bottom, twisting into shapes I dared not name. A warning, she called it. But what use are omens to the dead?"

~ The Haunting of Blackwood Manor

"Are you sure that an hour will be enough time?" Sofia asked as she pulled the company's luxury SUV to a stop outside a stately mansion in the exclusive Vaucluse area.

After a brief discussion with Jared over breakfast, Emily had contacted the current owners to arrange a meeting under the pretense of compiling material on Victor Barrow's life to accompany the auction catalog. As long as she could access all the areas she needed to, an hour would be plenty.

Climbing out of the air-conditioned vehicle and into the late morning sunshine, Emily's conviction wilted a little. In the aftermath of last night's storm, her plan had seemed plausible.

But now, in the harsh clarity of daylight, doubt crept in. Victor had been dead for over thirty years. Did she really think any trace of him would still remain within those walls?

And yet, she clung to the hope that something of him might linger there. After all, Emily knew she'd left imprints of herself behind in her Seattle apartment—faint echoes of emotion and memory etched into the spaces she had called home. She could only pray that Victor had done the same.

Stepping toward the wrought-iron gates that fanned the entry, she took a deep breath and pushed the button for the intercom. When she didn't get a response, Emily tried again but heard nothing other than the constant hum of cicadas, and the melodic warble of a nearby butcher bird. A trickle of perspiration ran down her spine as she pulled out her cell and dialed the home's occupants.

An older woman answered, "Hello. Is that you, Doug?"

"Mrs. Channing? It's Emily Sloane from Bell's Auctions. We spoke on the phone this morning."

"Oh." The woman sounded disappointed. "One moment."

The call ended abruptly, and Emily was left waiting by the padlocked gates, wondering if this had been a monumental mistake. A few minutes later, she heard the distinct crunch of gravel on the path and saw a petite woman tottering toward her from behind a row of hedges. She was eighty if she was a day, and dressed stylishly in a light blue linen dress, her wispy silver hair drawn back into an elegant bun at her nape. Emily could only wish she was as fashionable at that age.

"Sorry to keep you waiting, dear. I'm afraid the gate must be manually unlocked at the moment." She took a key from her pocket and inserted it into the padlock, turning it with ease. "That blasted storm last night knocked the power out. No offense, but I was rather hoping you were the repairman."

"None taken." Emily smiled at her. "And thank you for agreeing to see me on such short notice. I promise not to take up too much of your time."

Following Mrs. Channing through the expansive, rain-soaked garden, Emily stopped with a jolt as the two-story Italianate house emerged from behind the sprawling branches of a large and rather familiar weeping fig. It was eerily identical to the one in her nightmare, right down to the gnarled tree roots she'd stumbled over during the dream.

"Magnificent, isn't she?" Mrs. Channing said, her voice laced with admiration as she admired the stately tree. "I'm so glad she weathered the storm unscathed."

"Can't say the same for us," grumbled a voice from the doorway. Emily peered around Mrs. Channing to find an older man leaning on a mahogany cane.

"Poor dear," Mrs. Channing tutted. "Ray's arthritis plays up terribly in this weather. Ray, we have company. This is Emily from the auction house."

She raised a hand in greeting. "Pleased to meet you, Mr. Channing."

He observed her for a long moment, his silence heavy and unnerving, and Emily felt herself shrinking under his intense scrutiny.

"I'll put the kettle on," he said finally, turning and vanishing through the shadowed doorway.

"We'll take tea in the garden," Mrs. Channing said lightly. "It's such a nice day."

Torn between offering to help and not wanting to intrude, Emily followed the older woman around the side of the house to a quaint little patio that reminded her of a scene from a period drama. Beneath a trellis of pale pink climbing roses, an old-fashioned white iron garden setting was laid out with a pitcher of iced water that was already beading with condensation. "Please, help yourself," Mrs. Channing told her. "I'll be back with our tea."

Emily gratefully poured herself a glass, the chilled water a welcome relief from the stifling heat. But rather than take a seat, she wandered to the edge of the patio, her gaze sweeping the garden for a marble pedestal large enough to support Barrow's life-sized hound. If her dream held any truth, it would be around the other side of the house—if it still existed at all.

Mrs. Channing arrived with a tea tray laden with delicate china cups, a matching pot, and a small plate of cookies, her husband in tow. "Lavender shortbread," she announced proudly as she poured the tea. "Freshly baked this morning."

Ray eased himself slowly into a chair, watching as Emily stirred a couple of sugar cubes into her cup.

"Are you not sweet enough, love?" He arched a bushy brow, and heat crept up Emily's neck. But before she could form a response, he gave her a cheeky wink and shoveled three cubes into his own tea. "Nevermind. Me neither."

Emily bit back a laugh but averted her eyes from his cup. The milky liquid resembled dishwater, and it turned her stomach just to see it. Instead, she lifted her head to admire the fragrant blooms twisting through the trellis above. "You have such a charming garden. I could imagine it would be quite the task to look after."

"Thank you, dear. And it is. We have to employ a full-time gardener these days to keep it under control. Plus, it's also helpful to have someone on the grounds often."

"For security?"

Mrs. Channing gave a crisp nod.

"Have you had issues with Barrow's fans poking around?" Emily asked, taking a cookie. Her hosts exchanged a glance, and Ray settled deeper into his chair with a considering look.

"So, you've heard the rumors then."

Emily bit into the shortbread, the bright flavors of lavender and lemon bursting on her tongue, momentarily distracting her. She swallowed and brushed a few stray crumbs from her lap. "What rumors would they be, Mr. Channing?"

"We both know why you're here, love. So quit beating around the bush and just spit it out." His bushy brows lifted in challenge. "You won't offend me. I'm an old man."

Emily stared at him, perplexed. She wasn't sure if he was making light of the situation or if she should be the one taking offense. Australians could be a sarcastic lot, and she hadn't been able to get a read on a single one yet. Jared especially.

"Very well." Emily took a deep breath, choosing her words carefully. "I've been in the country less than a week and know very little about Victor Barrow. I'd like to include some interesting backstory for the auction catalog and was hoping you'd allow me to take a look at his writing room. See if I can get a feel for what it might have been like for him back in the day."

Ray snorted. "If you're after that missing manuscript, you're wasting your time. Your lot already gave it a thorough going over."

If by "your lot" he meant Bell's, he was probably referring to an appraisal done decades earlier—long before her time. She couldn't speak to what had been missed or discovered back then.

But she did know one thing: no one read a room—or an object—the way she could.

"That's not my intent," she assured him. "I'd just like to immerse myself in his former surroundings. Look around and see what he saw—that sort of thing. I believe the statue of the Hound was visible from his desk. Is that correct?"

Mrs. Channing gave a visible shudder. "Awful thing. So glad we had that removed after that fellow—" She broke off, her lips pressing into a thin line.

Emily glanced at Ray to see him giving his wife a pointed look.

"After what, Mrs. Channing?"

The older woman suddenly seemed very interested in the bottom of her teacup.

Ray let out a weary sigh. "We found someone in the garden late one evening. Young chap. Trying to pry the statue off the marble, and with a bloody screwdriver would you believe! I confronted him, and he claimed he worked for Barrow. Looked high as a bloody kite, if you ask me. Had this wild look about him, and he kept rambling about something Victor left for him."

Mrs. Channing gave a nervous little shake of her head. "That was enough for us. The statue always gave me the creeps, but after that night... I didn't want it anywhere near the house."

Ray nodded. "The estate's executor had originally listed it as a retained asset, meaning it had to stay with the property. But once we explained the situation, they signed off on a quick transfer. Bell's took it off our hands—saved us the trouble of listing it ourselves."

Emily's pulse ticked faster. Could it have been someone from Pendleton, or even Simon Reed?

"Did he threaten you?" she asked.

"Nothing like that. I called the police, of course, but they couldn't do anything. He was long gone before they turned up."

Emily retrieved her phone from her purse and quickly brought up a headshot of Reed. "Do you think this could be him?" she asked Ray.

The older man peered at her screen over the top of his glasses. "Could have been. It was over twenty years ago. And he certainly wasn't wearing that tweed coat when he broke in here. Who is he, then?"

"His name is Simon Reed. He was rumored to have been brought on by Barrow's publishers to ghostwrite for him while his health was declining."

"Ghostwrite?" Mrs. Channing gave a theatrical shudder. "Sounds decidedly gothic. Whatever does that mean?"

Emily turned to her. "It's industry speak for an author who writes under another's name while claiming to be said author."

"Oh my. Is that even legal?"

"As long as both parties agree. It's more common than you would think."

"So, that fellow might've been telling the truth after all," Ray mused, rubbing his chin.

Emily shrugged, setting down her cup. "I guess we'll never know."

Mrs. Channing gave her a warm smile. "Would you like to have a look inside now, dear? Ray can show you through while I clear all this away."

"That would be wonderful. But please, let me help." Emily reached across the table, gathering the empty cups and saucers, but froze as she shifted her own, the pattern in the bottom of the teacup stopping her cold.

The dark leaves had drifted into a vague shape—long-limbed, crouched low, as if ready to pounce. Its head was turned, as though it knew it was being watched. The image was crude, but unmistakable. Not coincidental. Not random.

A chill slid down her spine.

She blinked, then looked again, but the shape held. *Not a vision then.* She didn't know whether to be relieved or concerned. It was only discarded tea leaves...

Her instincts, however, whispered otherwise. This wasn't nothing. It was a sign.

The Hound was calling.

It was easy to dismiss omens in the daylight. Inside the Channings' home, where sunlight spilled through tall windows and laughter echoed faintly from down the hall, the weight of her unease felt distant—like a bad dream shrugged off with the morning.

Emily hadn't known what to expect—she'd only glimpsed Victor's study as it had been in the early nineties, cobwebbed and cloaked in shadows, through the haze of a vision. But the reality was startlingly different. There were no dark corridors, no oppressive hush. Just white-washed walls, simple artwork, and polished floorboards that gleamed beneath her feet.

A house once steeped in macabre legend now breathed light and life. The contrast was jarring—and oddly comforting. It was hard to imagine it as the same place where Barrow had once worked, surrounded by the ghosts of his own imagination.

"I'm not sure this will be of any help. It's just a guest room now," Ray said, opening a door and stepping aside.

Emily drew in a slow breath to ready herself and stepped past him.

He wasn't wrong.

Gone was Victor's imposing desk and the precarious towers of books. Instead, a queen-sized bed dominated the space, its floral quilt carefully tucked. The dark timber bookcases had been painted a soft peach to match the decor, and were styled with trailing plants, knick-knacks, and framed photos of the Channing family. Emily's fingers brushed the shelf where, in her vision, she'd seen a portrait of Victor's wife, Florence. Now, in its place, sat an empty gin bottle spouting a lush cascade of Devil's Ivy.

She turned toward the French doors, moving to where the desk had once been. If she closed her eyes, she could almost see Victor hunched over the notebook, ink-stained fingers dragging through his hair. But the gauzy lace curtains diffused the daylight, blurring the outside world, making it impossible to see what he might have seen.

"Has the view from here changed much since you bought the house?" she asked, her voice hushed.

Ray, who had settled onto the bench seat at the foot of the bed, heaved a grunt as he pushed himself upright and shuffled toward her side. Guilt prickled at Emily for making him move, but he waved off her concern, motioning toward the doors with his cane.

"Go on, have a look," he said.

She turned the glass knob and pushed the doors open, stepping out into a small courtyard. In the center of the well-manicured lawn was a small, rounded garden.

Ray pointed at it with his cane. "Dottie put some shrubs around the old pedestal after that mess with the trespasser. Figured the bees would keep any more troublemakers at bay."

Emily stepped closer, her gaze sharpening as she reached the circular patch of greenery. A neatly clipped hedge of Chinese Box now enclosed the marble block, its once-noble purpose reduced to a mere plinth for a cracked Grecian urn overflowing with cheerful blooms. But Emily barely noticed the flowers.

Now that she stood before it, she could clearly picture the statue of the great hound. More than that—she could see Barrow, somehow sprawled across it in the throes of heart failure. But could a man in his seventies really have scaled that pedestal? Could he have clung to the bronze beast long enough to die upon it?

Logic wavered, and her body betrayed her with a ripple of unease. The memory of last night's nightmare pressed at the edge of her mind—not just a dream, but something heavier, more rooted. She'd felt Barrow's panic. His heartbeat had thundered in her own chest. She hadn't just seen him die...

She'd been him.

Emily exhaled sharply and gave her head a subtle shake, as if she could dislodge the weight pressing in around her thoughts. *This wasn't how her visions usually worked.* She kept telling herself that. Kept pretending she was unfazed. But the edges were fraying, and no amount of composure could fully hide the fact that it was beginning to rattle her.

"Would you mind if I stepped in for a closer look, Mr. Channing?" she asked lightly, gesturing toward the pedestal. "Sometimes being in the space helps me get a better feel for things. I won't disturb anything, I promise."

Ray waved a dismissive hand. "Knock yourself out. I'll be inside, where it's cooler."

She watched him shuffle back indoors before turning her attention back to the pedestal. Picking her way carefully among the plants, she pressed her palm against the cold marble, bracing for whatever it had to tell her.

But it remained silent as the grave.

Disappointed, she swept her fingers across the surface, brushing away debris and leaf litter left behind by the storm. All that remained of the Hound were four rusted holes, pocking the stone like forgotten wounds—ghosts of the bolts that once held it fast.

She dipped her finger into one—then jerked back with a sharp gasp as pain lanced through her palm, deep and sudden. Emily yanked her hand away, expecting to find a bee sting, or a thorn embedded in her skin. But there was nothing. No sting, no puncture, no sign of redness at all. And yet, she had felt it—the unmistakable bite of something slamming through tender flesh. She sucked in a breath, rubbing at the phantom ache as a voice—thin, urgent—echoed in her mind.

"It's got to be here... He said he would leave it for me."

Her pulse quickened. Someone—possibly Simon Reed—had searched this very spot, desperate to find something hidden beneath the statue. Desperate enough to try prying it off with a screwdriver.

Emily rubbed at her palm again, the sharp tearing ache making sense. The pain hadn't been just residual energy—it was a memory, someone else's memory. A violent one.

The rumors about the missing manuscript no longer felt like literary myth—they felt alarmingly real. Tangible. As though its resting place could be within the pedestal itself.

And yet... something tugged at her.

The vision she'd seen—Barrow, writing frantically, felt raw. Final. Maybe even personal. If what was hidden here *wasn't* the manuscript, what had Barrow really been trying to leave behind?

And who had he meant it for?

5

The Weight of Secrets

*"Some secrets are left to rot in shallow
graves. Others press heavy upon the soul,
each day a slow strangulation. But the worst
are those written in the eyes of a man who
will never tell you the truth."*
~ The Blight on Blackwood Heath

Back in the auction rooms, Emily sat at her desk, laptop open, absently chewing on a fingernail. By some miracle, she'd tracked down the stonemason who had supplied the marble block for the Hound—a charming, retired fellow who regaled her with a wealth of stories, including how Florence Barrow had also commissioned him to prepare the couple's gravestones well in advance. Emily had shuddered at the morbidity but concluded that it was indeed thoughtful planning on Florence's behalf. Unfortunately, he also informed her that the pedestal did not contain a secret compartment; it was simply a regular Carrara block with a bit of decorative edging, and nothing more.

"So why was Reed so intent on prying the statue off it?" she pondered aloud. The question gnawed at her, a puzzle piece that refused to fit.

She knew she should let sleeping dogs lie, especially given the stonemason's clear-cut explanation. Yet, the morning's revelations had only sharpened her resolve. Barrow's legacy, combined with Reed's mysterious, unfinished search, had drawn her into a web of intrigue far greater than she had ever expected. Each step forward seemed to uncover an extra layer of complexity, and the thought of turning back now felt impossible.

With her pulse quickening and her excitement mounting, Emily realized she was standing at the threshold of a discovery that could change everything. And she was determined to press on, no matter the cost.

Leaving her office, she raced downstairs, not bothering to wait for the lift, and stopped by Sofia's desk.

"Sorry, Em. He's in back-to-back meetings until at least six," Sofia told her with an apologetic smile. "Want me to leave a message?"

Emily hesitated, exhaling through her nose. *Damn it*. She didn't want to wait, but interrupting Jared right now would do no good. "No, I'll catch him later. Thanks," she said, forcing a smile. Time was slipping away. If she couldn't talk to Jared about it first, she'd have to do the next best thing—go straight to Reed herself.

Emily climbed the stairs to the acquisitions department, hoping to catch Carmel at her desk. But the sight of the older woman buried beneath precarious stacks of catalogs, antique price guides, and towering paperwork sent an unexpected prickle down her spine. Victor Barrow had been like this in her vision. Hidden. Surrounded. Hunched over his own mountain of books and papers, consumed by something that had followed him to his grave.

She took a fortifying breath and slipped into the chair across from Carmel. "You look busy," she noted.

Still tapping away at her computer, Carmel barely spared Emily a glance. "I'm always busy leading up to an auction. What do you need?"

Emily leaned in, lowering her voice. "I need to set up a meeting with Simon Reed."

That got her attention. Carmel stopped typing, removed her glasses, and settled those shrewd brown eyes on Emily. Her gaze was sharp and discerning, missing nothing—not details, not hesitations, not the opportunities lurking in plain sight. Though diminutive in stature, Carmel Vega carried herself with an assurance that made her presence feel twice its size. "Why?"

Emily chose her words carefully. "I want to ask him about his time working with Barrow. It could add depth to the catalog."

Carmel arched a skeptical brow. "And?"

Emily blew out a sigh. "And I think he knows more than he's letting on."

Carmel studied her for a long moment before shaking her

head. "Reed's been hounding us for years to let him see Barrow's statue. He's persistent—I'll tell you that."

"Why not just let him have a look, then? If you were planning on holding back the sale until Barrow's anniversary, what potential harm could it have done?"

Carmel sighed, rubbing her temple. "Much of our inventory is kept secret until it goes to auction. It's just the way we work. Private sellers and estates expect discretion, and some pieces—especially those with complicated provenance—are held indefinitely until legal matters are settled." She hesitated, then added, "Besides, we can't afford the precedent. If we start bending the rules for one person, we'll have collectors and academics crawling all over us, demanding access."

"Which is exactly why I should meet with him. I'll be discreet and I'll find out what he's after."

Carmel frowned, tapping her fingers against her desk. "I want to help you, Emily, but Jared would never sign off on this."

Emily dropped her voice. "Jared doesn't have to know."

A hint of a smile played on Carmel's full, dark red lips. "I think I like this side of you," she mused. "Bold, secretive, verging on irresponsible..."

"I prefer *determined*."

Carmel let out a chuckle before her expression sobered. "Look, I get it. You're young, and eager to prove yourself, and honestly? I respect that. But don't be stupid about it." She reached for her keyboard, entering a few keystrokes before scrolling through a list of contacts. "Reed might be nothing more than a harmless horror writer, but he's been circling this auction like a vulture. Whatever he's after, it's not just for the sake of nostalgia."

"Exactly! I've been all over the estate ledger and there's zero info on the statue. Reed knows something we don't. I can taste it. Please, Carmel. I'll be nothing but professional," Emily said.

"I don't doubt that." Carmel grabbed a notepad and scrawled something down before sliding it across the desk. "His last known address is in Redfern, and this is the phone number I have on file. Shouldn't be too hard to get a hold of him."

Emily reached for the slip of paper, but Carmel didn't let go just yet. "One more thing," she said. "Don't let him talk his way into an early inspection. He'll get his chance before the bidding starts, and we don't need him poking around before then."

Emily frowned. "I wasn't planning to."

Carmel finally let go of the paper. "Just... watch your step, alright?"

Emily nodded, slipping the note into her pocket. "Understood."

As she left the office, the weight of the paper felt heavier than it should.

Simon Reed was still searching for answers. And now, so was she.

Simon Reed chose a secluded cafe on the city's fringe for their meeting—neutral ground, close enough to Bell's, but far enough away to avoid unwanted eyes or ears. The place was old-fashioned, with checkered floors and a long, glass-fronted counter lined with sandwiches, rolls, and—best of all—bagels. Emily doubted they'd compare with her favorites from Capitol Hill, but she was keen to find out.

She spotted him the moment she stepped inside. He sat at a corner table—a slightly older version of his author photo—his posture rigid, fingers drumming against the ceramic of his untouched coffee. His sharp gaze flicked toward the entrance, narrowing as she approached.

Emily squared her shoulders and crossed the room. "Mr. Reed?" she greeted him, slipping her purse from her shoulder and extending her hand.

He didn't respond right away; instead, he studied her with an assessing look that made it clear he hadn't yet decided whether she was an obstacle or an opportunity.

"You're from Bell's." It wasn't a question.

"I am," Emily confirmed, taking the seat opposite him and withdrawing her tablet. "And thank you for agreeing to see me. I'm very keen to learn more about the work you did for Victor Barrow."

"Learn more?" Reed sat back with a chuckle. "How about you start by telling me whatever it is you think you know, plus what's in it for me?"

"Very well," Emily conceded, tapping the screen to bring up

the photos she'd taken of the pedestal in the Channings' garden. She turned the tablet toward him. "To be completely honest, I know very little. But I believe we can help each other. You see, I know that you've been trying to get in touch with us for some time about gaining access to The Hound of Blackwood Vale statue."

He glanced at the screen, barely giving the images more than a cursory look, but something flickered in his expression—reluctance, or maybe something closer to recognition. He shook his head. "This means nothing to me."

"It's the marble block that the Hound was affixed to when it was still part of Barrow's estate."

His eyes slid to hers. "I know what it is."

Emily leaned in. "So it was you in the garden that night," she said, leveling the accusation directly at him.

Reed's eyes widened, and for a moment, he looked like a deer caught in headlights. "What are you talking about?"

She smirked, feeling a surge of confidence. "Don't play dumb, Simon. I know you tried to pry the statue off. What I'm most curious about, is why."

Reed clenched his jaw, his fingers curling into a fist on the table. "That's my own business. And you have no proof that was me."

Faster than a viper, she reached across the small table and snagged his wrist. "You injured your hand though, didn't you, Simon?" she asked sweetly. It was a punt on her behalf, but the way Reed's eyes flared confirmed her hunch. "If I'm not mistaken, the screwdriver you were using slipped and tore your palm. I bet you have a nasty scar there."

"I don't know what you're talking about," he said haughtily, the tremor in his voice a thin crack in his facade.

She studied him openly, concluding that, for some unknown reason, Simon Reed was terrified.

"Why do you want the statue so badly?"

"I don't," he snapped, trying to pull his wrist from her grip.

Emily released him carefully, her fingers deliberately grazing his gold watch as she sat back. Images immediately danced in her mind.

> *Candles flicker atop a table set for two. Soft music plays in the background. A pretty brunette—her brown eyes wide with admiration—reaches forward, a black box in her open palm.*

She let out a small gasp. "Your wife gave you that watch, didn't she, Simon?" she asked before she could think better of it. "For your twenty-fifth birthday. There's an inscription on the back." Her eyes narrowed as her memory focused on what she'd just seen. *"Write your own way."*

Simon Reed scrambled out of his seat so quickly it fell backward onto the floor with a clatter. "Who the hell are you?"

"Mr. Reed."

"How did you know that?"

"Simon. Please, sit down."

"Dad?"

Emily turned to see a young woman approaching their table, brows drawn together in concern. She wore a serving apron and a name tag that read "Briony." Her dark eyes, so like the ones in Emily's vision, flicked between them before settling on her father. "Everything okay?"

Reed sighed, rubbing a hand over his face. "It's fine, sweetheart. We were just talking."

Briony didn't look convinced. Clearly aware of her concern, Reed waved a dismissive hand. "Go back to work. I'll be out of your way soon."

Emily picked up a menu. "Actually, I'm famished." She gave Reed a look that said she was prepared to stay all day if it meant she'd get the information she wanted. "I'd kill for a cream cheese bagel. Toasted. And a large black coffee to go. Thank you."

The tension lingered as Briony hesitated, then finally gave Emily a wary glance before retreating to the counter.

Reed picked up his chair and sat back down. "What do you want from me?" he hissed.

"The truth."

"About what?"

"The night Barrow died and the Hound's role in it."

Reed paled but put on a show of looking baffled. "He had a heart attack at his desk."

"Perhaps he did. But just like how I knew about your watch, Simon, I know things. And I know Victor was being hounded by something, or *someone*, right before his death." She leaned forward. "He was scared, wasn't he? Much like you are right now. I'm willing to help you get what you want, but I also need answers."

"I thought you said you were from the auction house."

"I am," Emily told him again.

"What are you, then? A psychic?" He huffed out a shaky laugh.

Emily gave a small, knowing smile. "Something like that."

"Christ." He dragged a hand over his cropped hair. "Is that even legal?"

"It's why I was hired."

He narrowed his eyes. "I could expose you, you know."

She met his gaze, steady and calm. "You could try. But no one would believe you." A beat. "Trust me—I should know."

Reed scowled. "Fine. You get me an inspection, and you'll get your answers."

"That's not how this works. I can't just grant early inspections on a whim. The viewing is scheduled, and if you're serious about bidding—"

He let out a soft, incredulous laugh, shaking his head. "You clearly don't know what you're dealing with. This is about more than just the goddamn statue." He looked to where his daughter was busy preparing what Emily hoped was her bagel. "It's the key to everything."

Emily considered him, weighing his agitation against her own curiosity. Whatever he was after, it was obvious that it also affected his family.

She tapped the screen of her tablet, shutting off the display. "Fine. I'll arrange for you to see the Hound."

Reed glanced back at her sharply, surprised.

"But on my terms and under strict supervision," she added. "And whatever you're hoping to find—you don't touch anything unless I say so."

He exhaled, some of the tension in his frame easing, but his eyes still burned with something unreadable.

"Deal."

6

A Midnight Caller

By the time Jared strode into the restaurant, just shy of seven, Emily had already been there long enough to second-guess the entire evening. She'd taken a cab—wisely, as it turned out. Her nerves had needed something to take the edge off, and the crisp semillon she'd ordered had turned into two by the time she spotted him weaving through the crowd.

She watched as his gaze swept the room and landed on her. Composed on the outside, she drained the last sip from her glass, set it down with practiced calm, and rose to greet him.

"Well, this is unexpected," he said with an easy grin, leaning in to press a slow, deliberate kiss to her cheek. Stolen moments such as those were few and far between, and she relished in the tenderness of his touch, in the trace of his cologne—spiced cedar and something unmistakably *Jared*. Which was a mistake, of course. His scent, combined with the wine, flooded her senses, making her momentarily forget why she had called him there in the first place.

She recovered herself, somewhat reluctantly, and drew a breath. Holding his gaze, she let just the hint of a smile curve her lips. "I've been doing a little digging."

He rubbed his chin, eyes narrowing with interest. "Of course you have."

She searched his expression for any trace of disappointment but found none. If anything, there was something else in his eyes—admiration.

Encouraged, she pressed on. "I managed to get a meeting with the owners of Barrow's estate this morning," she added, lifting her glass.

There was the briefest pause in his expression—enough to clock the timing—but not a hint of judgment. Just a small, knowing smile, as if he'd already expected her to move quickly.

Alex would've made a performance of it, demanded details, asserted control.

But Jared? He simply waited, patient as ever, giving her the space to lay everything out.

So she did.

They shifted to a table tucked into a quiet corner, where the low lighting softened the edges of the bustling dining room. Jared ordered a glass of red, while Emily, already feeling the effects of the wine she'd had earlier, asked for sparkling water instead.

Over the course of their meal, she laid it all out—her visit with the Channings, the unwelcome visitor in the garden, Mrs. Channing's reaction to the statue, and the strange sensation she'd had when touching the pedestal. Jared listened quietly, his expression serious.

When she finally paused, he sat back, wiped his mouth with a napkin, and regarded her with a thoughtful tilt of his head.

"So, you think the Channings' intruder was Simon Reed?"

She nodded, careful not to reveal too much. Reed hadn't outright confessed, but he hadn't denied it either. And she knew the truth well enough.

"Who else would it have been? He's the only one who's been chasing the statue all these years."

She considered telling Jared about her meeting with Reed—but the words caught in her throat. Not that she wanted to keep it from him. She just wasn't ready to see that flicker of concern in his eyes, to hear the inevitable warning in his voice.

Jared leaned forward, his expression grave. "So... do you still think he killed Barrow for the manuscript?"

"No." Emily shook her head, resolute. "I'm beginning to think Barrow might have left it for him."

Jared frowned. "But why all the secrecy and theatrics with the statue—why not just give it to him outright?"

"Because he didn't entirely trust Reed. Because it's Victor Barrow—Master of the Macabre. Nothing was ever straightforward with him. Even his death."

"And you think Reed knows where the manuscript is?"

"I think he *thinks* he does. If I'm right, he's already tried to remove the statue once, and now he's asking for a private inspection. He's not interested in the pedestal—which, according to the stonemason who carved it, is nothing but a solid block of marble, anyway. That leaves the Hound."

Jared ran a hand over his jaw, eyes narrowing. "But the sculpture was a gift, wasn't it? Commissioned by Barrow's wife?"

"Exactly. And a surprise, from what I can gather. Which means she had no reason to build in some secret compartment. If something *is* inside it, it wasn't part of her design. Barrow must have had it altered later."

Jared blew out a breath. "Christ. That changes everything. Do we know who made the statue?"

"Vik and I went through the estate ledger and found the original invoice from an Italian foundry. But it was basically useless. Just a vague entry—'standing hellhound, bronze' or something like that—and a record of the commission. No design specs, no artisan details. Nothing we can trace."

Jared leaned back in his chair, gaze steady. "So—a dead end."

"Well... yes and no."

His brow lifted. "Meaning?"

Emily leaned forward, her voice low. "Remember the very

first flash I had when touching the statue in the storeroom? Barrow was writing. Fast, intense, like he was racing against the clock. He wasn't tucking pages into a hollow sculpture—he was trying to get something *out*."

Jared frowned. "And you think it was the manuscript?"

"I don't know," she admitted. "It *felt* important—like it could be the manuscript. But it could've just as easily been a letter to Pendleton, or a deathbed confession... even a will. But here's the thing—whatever Barrow was trying to say, I don't think he ever got the chance to finish it. The Hound keeps showing me the same thing, but nothing about hiding or sealing something away. I can't grasp any sense of purpose—just overwhelming urgency." She shook her head, frustrated.

Jared eyed her carefully. "So, what's our next step?"

"Simon Reed," she insisted. "He was closer to Barrow in those final weeks than anyone. If there's something left unsaid—something Barrow's editor couldn't publish, or wouldn't—then Reed's the only one who might recognize it. Or maybe even be the reason for it."

"You want to bring him in early." Jared rubbed his jaw—a classic sign he was thinking about her idea.

She paused, not wanting to rush him. "We're stewards now, Jay. If Barrow left something behind—something meant to be seen—we owe it to him to see it through."

His gaze sharpened slightly. Not skeptical, but serious.

"This isn't about headlines. I know that's not what drives you. But if we wait until this thing's on the block and someone opens it with a crowbar in front of a crowd—what happens if it's personal? Or worse, if it was never meant to be public at all?"

A beat of silence passed between them. Then Jared gave a slow nod.

"Shall I get Carmel to set up a meeting?"

"No. She has enough on her plate. I'll call him myself."

"Okay." Emily exhaled, trying not to show her relief. But if Reed mentioned he'd cleared it with her already, things could get awkward fast. Still, it wasn't worth stressing over now. She'd deal with that later. And only if she had to.

Jared lifted his glass. "Well. Looks like you've been handling things just fine without me."

Here comes the reprimand. The reminder that her role was to verify provenance—not chase ghosts or stir up scandal. *Not make deals on the side.*

"I'm just doing what I was hired to do," she said quickly, already bracing for pushback.

But Jared just shook his head, a faint smile tugging at the corner of his mouth as he leaned in. "You still don't get it, do you?"

Emily frowned. Twice today, she'd been told that—but his gaze lingered, something heated flickering in its depths. She tried to focus on her meal, but her appetite had vanished. Mouth suddenly dry, she reached for her glass, but Jared's hand closed over hers.

"When you accepted my job offer that night in the Jacuzzi, do you remember what I told you?"

His thumb began tracing slow, deliberate circles over her knuckles. Of course she remembered. It was the night that changed everything. The way his eyes had lingered on her lips. *That kiss.* How could she forget?

She raised her gaze to him. His usually twinkling blue eyes were dark, steady, fathomless.

"I meant what I said, Em."

A slow shiver ran through her, pooling deep in her core. He'd told her he'd been attracted to her. He'd told her...

"We make a great team." Jared's fingers tightened around hers, lifting them from her glass to press against his burning lips. The restaurant, the dim candlelight, the murmur of distant conversations—all of it faded into the background.

"We make a great team," he repeated, his voice lower now, rougher.

Emily swallowed hard, heat creeping up her neck. She knew she should say something—laugh it off, change the subject, remind herself that this was dangerous—but she couldn't. The air between them had shifted, thick with something undeniable, something that had been simmering for far too long.

They left almost immediately. The drive back to the loft was silent, but the tension between them felt anything but.

Emily sat with her hands folded in her lap, her skin still burning where Jared had kissed her. The streetlights flickered past in a blur as Jared sped his Porsche out of the city and presumably toward The Rocks and home. Emily didn't care. Her awareness was pinned to the man beside her—the steady grip of his fingers on the wheel, the subtle bob of his Adam's apple when he swallowed.

Jared's left hand rested on the gearshift, loose and close. Too close. Close enough that if she so much as shifted, his hand would brush her thigh.

She didn't move.

Not because she didn't want to, but because she knew what would happen if she did.

Jared flicked her a glance as they passed beneath a streetlamp, his eyes narrowing slightly—not with disapproval, exactly, but with calculation. "You really told the Channings you were handling estate logistics?"

Emily didn't flinch. "Technically, I *am* verifying provenance. I just didn't mention it wasn't my official role to request access."

He let out a low chuckle, shaking his head. "You know," he said, voice edged with something she couldn't quite place, "I never expected you to be quite this defiant."

Emily arched a brow. "Defiant?"

His smirk was slow, deliberate. "Confident. Unapologetic. Talking your way into a private meeting under false pretenses—working outside your scope like it's the most natural thing in the world. Whether or not I approve." He exhaled, his gaze drifting to her mouth before returning to the road. "It's... unexpected."

She swallowed, her pulse a steady drum against her ribs. "You don't like it?"

Jared didn't answer right away, and when he finally did, his voice was even lower, rougher. "Oh, I think I do."

Something had flickered in his expression—something dark and wanting—and before she could talk herself out of it, she leaned across and brushed the lightest kiss against his jaw.

Jared stilled, his breath catching. A beat of silence stretched between them, then, in a low, almost breathless voice, he murmured, "That's not fair."

Without another word, he steered the car toward the curb and cut the engine. The sudden quiet only amplified the tension thrumming between them.

His fingers flexed against the steering wheel.

"Get out."

Emily blinked, certain she'd misheard. "Sorry—what?"

Jared didn't look at her. His jaw was clenched, eyes locked straight ahead. "Get. Out. Of. The. Car."

Her pulse kicked. In one awful beat, she realized she'd misjudged everything—the warm glances, the lingering touches, the way he always stood just a little too close—and now she'd crossed a line she hadn't meant to.

"Okay," she said slowly, voice cooler than she felt. Her fingers fumbled for her purse, the door clicking open.

The night air hit her like a slap—dense, humid, thick with regret. She stepped onto the curb, heart thudding, barely registering the way her body shook. The street was quiet. Dark. Unfamiliar.

She turned back toward the car.

And found Jared already there. Standing between her and the

passenger door, the heat of him impossibly close.

"Jay—" she started, but the words dissolved the moment his hand found her waist, anchoring her.

The other lifted to her jaw, steady, warm. He tilted her chin until their eyes locked, and for the first time since he'd spoken, she saw the emotion that had been simmering underneath: not anger. Not annoyance.

Restraint.

"Do you have any idea," he said, voice low and ragged, "what it's like trying to stay professional around you?"

She didn't answer. Couldn't. Not with the way his thumb brushed over her cheek, not with the look in his eyes like he was already halfway ruined.

Then he kissed her.

And it wasn't careful. It wasn't slow.

It was the kind of kiss that made her forget her name.

This wasn't testing the waters. This was raw, unavoidable fate, catching up to them like a tidal wave, crushing and inescapable.

When they finally pulled apart, their foreheads touching, and the sound of their ragged breaths filling the space between them, Emily's world narrowed to this moment, to only him.

"Are we really doing this?" she whispered, fingers splayed against the solid heat of his chest to steady herself.

Jared's smirk was unmistakable, but there was something deeper beneath it this time—something certain.

"Oh, we're definitely doing this."

The elevator doors had barely closed when Jared caught her around the waist and backed her against the mirrored wall, his mouth finding hers with a hunger that had simmered all evening. Emily responded instantly, her fingers pulling his already half-unbuttoned shirt from his trousers and sliding her hands under the fabric, finding the warm skin beneath.

The confined space amplified everything: the soft hitch in her breath, the low groan he gave when her nails grazed his chest. His hands roamed her sides, urgent but reverent, as if relearning every inch—the experience significantly more satisfying than the kiss in the hot tub.

The ding of the elevator jolted them apart, breathless. Jared straightened, shirt gaping open, lips parted, eyes dark.

Without a word, he took her hand and guided her forward, his palm pressed firmly to the small of her back, his breath still hot against her neck as they stepped into the loft's tiny foyer. Emily's pulse hammered. Her skin felt too tight, every nerve lit from within.

He fumbled with the keycard—his fingers clumsy in a way that made her want to drag him back into the elevator. They'd barely survived the car ride. If the night continued at this pace, survival was hardly guaranteed.

The lock clicked open. And a low, guttural growl rumbled

from the darkness beyond the door, slicing through the moment like a knife.

Lucy.

Emily barely had time to react before the massive black dog burst through the open door, nearly knocking Jared to the floor as she rushed past.

"Lucy! What the—" Jared lunged for her collar, but she was too quick, her sleek fur bristling, ears pinned flat against her skull. She threw herself against the door to the fire stairs, her snarls raw and unrelenting.

Emily's blood ran cold as Lucy's growls turned to frenzied, clipped barks. With a desperate, high-pitched whine, her claws raked the door, digging into the wood.

Beside her, Jared stiffened. "Something's got her spooked." His voice was low, wary. He flicked a glance at Emily, eyes dark with unease. "Stay inside."

Snatching Lucy's leash from the hook by the door, his movements were swift but calm, his jaw tight with focus. The dog strained against him, still on high alert, but he managed to clip the leash to her collar, murmuring low, soothing words that did little to calm the deep tremors running through her body.

Emily hovered near the doorway as he eased it open. A faint hum of emergency lighting flickered to life, casting eerie, wavering shadows as he stepped through. The heavy door groaned before slamming shut behind him, leaving her alone in the silence, her pulse thudding in her ears.

Minutes crawled by, each one stretching unbearably. Emily

busied herself with making a pot of tea, but the simple act did little to ease her mind. Instead, it brought the image in her tea leaves that morning, front and center—the dog. Had it truly been an omen?

Simon Reed already had a history of break and entering. Surely, he hadn't paid them an impromptu visit before she could secure access for him to see the Hound? The thought sent a chill through her, settling deep into her bones.

The click of the door made Emily flinch. Lucy shot into the room, nails skittering across the floor, and Jared followed close behind.

Relief hit hard and fast—so much so that her legs nearly buckled. Her first instinct was to cross the space between them and fall into his arms, but she didn't. He just stood there, with his shirt still open and damp with sweat. His hair was a mess, his jaw tight, but his eyes—sharp and so blue—met hers like a fuse to dry tinder.

She swallowed. "What happened?" Her voice came out tighter than she meant it to.

"Someone was definitely down there," Jared said, calm on the surface, but with steel beneath. "Luce tracked the scent down to the ground floor. But there's no forced entry. No sign of them now."

Emily dropped to her knees beside Lucy, running a hand along the dog's back, grounding herself in the warm, solid weight of her. "You scared them off, didn't you, girl?" she murmured. But even as she said it, she wasn't sure she believed it.

"Maybe." Jared didn't look convinced. He exhaled sharply, dragging a hand through his hair. "I'm calling security. I want to see if they picked up anything on the cameras."

"Good idea." She turned, forcing herself to focus on something other than the unease prickling at her skin. "I made some tea." She gestured to the pot steaming on the counter.

Jared's gaze softened—just for a moment. "Thanks," he said, but didn't make a move toward it. Instead, he leaned against the counter, arms crossed, eyes flicking toward the door. "Make mine extra strong." A ghost of a smirk touched his lips. "I don't plan on sleeping tonight."

Emily's pulse spiked.

"I'm not leaving you here alone," he added, quieter this time.

Of course, he probably meant that he'd be on the couch, monitoring the door. Not in her bed.

Still, the thought lingered, unbidden.

Emily nodded, turning to fill two mugs—because it gave her something to do, because if she kept looking at him, she might forget how to breathe. As he turned from her, phone pressed to his ear, the heat of his presence was still there, saturating the space between them. Protective. Fierce.

And far more dangerous than anything lurking outside.

7

Hidden in Plain Sight

"True concealment lies not in shadow, but in the ordinary. The most dreadful things are often dressed in dust and daylight—hiding not behind walls, but within them."

~ The Curse of Blackwood Bay

"Excuse us for a moment."

Emily had barely stepped into the meeting room when Jared caught her wrist—not rough, but firm. Intentional. His grip alone told her there was no room for debate. Before she could question it, he led her back into the hallway, the door clicking shut behind them.

Then he turned.

His hand planted on the wall beside her shoulder, boxing her in—not touching her, but close enough that she caught the sharp scent of his cologne. Her pulse stuttered.

Was he seriously doing this here? Now? Simon Reed and his

lawyer were waiting just on the other side of that door.

But the look on his face doused any illusion. This wasn't desire.

It was fury.

"You met with Reed yesterday?" His voice was low, too controlled, the edges honed with disappointment.

Her stomach dropped. *Shit.*

She opened her mouth to explain but faltered. The warmth in his eyes earlier that morning was gone—shuttered, locked away behind something sharper.

And just like that, the professional wall between them slammed back into place.

"Yeah. I made a call," she said, forcing calm into her voice. "Maybe it wasn't clean, but I was following the lead while it was still hot. If we'd waited—"

"You lied by omission." He cut her off with a scoff. "That's not a call, Emily. That's control."

The word hit her like a slap.

"I thought you liked me defiant," she shot back, flippant, out of self-defense.

His jaw flexed. "I do." He leaned in. Still not touching, but close enough that the heat of his frustration simmered between them. "But this isn't just defiance, Emily."

The use of her full name—sharp, clipped—sliced through her. Not because he was right. But because of the betrayal laced through it.

"You went to Reed behind my back. Promised him a look at

the Hound *before* we even agreed to bring him in. You don't see a problem with that?"

Her hands curled into fists at her sides. "I'm only doing exactly what you brought me here to do—I'm following the damn trail—and if that means finding answers without psychic intervention, then so be it. My instincts are all I've got when the visions run cold."

His hands balled into fists, matching hers. "You know I back your instincts. I always have. But you didn't even give me the chance to weigh in."

"Because I *knew* what you'd say," she hissed. "That I was out of line. That I should stay in my lane. But guess what? There is no lane with Barrow. It's all twisted, and fogged, and crawling with shadows. So forgive me for trying to feel my way through it."

"Jesus Christ, Em—you're not Trixie Belden."

She blinked at him. "Excuse me?"

"That means you don't go asking questions no one wants asked, stirring up ghosts. Hell, I'm surprised you don't have a map and a flashlight in your bag."

"Wow. That's where you're going with this?"

He didn't answer. Which was worse. Because that meant it was more than a careless remark.

"I'm not trying to keep you in a box," he admitted. "I just want to know when you're heading into the fire—*before* you're knee deep in it. I couldn't bear to see you get burned."

She pushed off the wall, shoulders squared—only to realize,

too late, that it meant her chest grazed his. The awareness sent heat licking down her spine, but she refused to let it show.

"I'm not trying to be reckless," she said, quieter now. "I'm trying to be effective. You want this auction to work? We need Reed. Like it or not, he might be the only person alive who knows exactly what that statue's hiding. And if it is Barrow's manuscript, then we're sitting on something priceless—and Reed wants it."

Jared's eyes darkened, his expression unreadable.

"That's leverage, Jay. I know it. You know it. And we can use it to our advantage."

His jaw worked. "After everything we learned last night," he said, voice dropping, "I can't rule out that he was the one who broke in."

Emily stilled. She'd seen the grainy footage from the security cameras—a hooded figure sprinting through the fire exit, too fast for a clean ID. The possibility that it had been Reed sent an icy trickle down her spine.

She swallowed. "We don't know that it was him. He's desperate, sure—but reckless? He's been circling this for *years*. Why blow it all now? He has a family to protect."

A beat of silence stretched between them as Jared clocked her mistake. She knew more about Simon Reed than she'd let on.

Finally, he exhaled and stepped back. "Fine," he muttered. "But if he so much as breathes wrong, I'm throwing him out on his ass."

Emily instantly relaxed, fighting the urge to smirk. "You

know, you're kind of hot when you go all alpha."

Jared's gaze dipped—first to her mouth, then her throat—then lower.

For one perfect second, the rest of the world—the manuscript, the argument, the risk—fell away.

Then Simon Reed's voice filtered through the door.

Jared scrubbed a hand through his hair and gestured toward the meeting room. "Let's get this over with."

Emily hesitated, heart still hammering, then pushed the door open.

The air in the room was tight, sour with the friction of unspoken arguments, the kind that brewed just beneath the surface. Emily felt it hit her like a pressure shift—an invisible weight pressing down.

Only this time, it was threefold.

First, there was the residual heat of her argument with Jared—still curling through her skin like static, unresolved and raw.

Then there was Simon Reed. A live wire pacing before her, restless energy bleeding through every clipped movement.

And finally, the auction itself—the unnerving awareness that history sat on the precipice, ready to tip one way or the other.

She swallowed, steadying herself.

Reed stopped pacing just long enough to glance at them—his gaze flitting between her and Jared, assessing. His lawyer barely shifted, arms crossed over the sleek lines of his tailored suit, disdain leaking from every pore.

A single, tense beat stretched between them.

Then there was a sharp click, followed by the rattle of the polished brass handle of the doors on the other side of the room. They flung open and a pair of Bell's security personnel strode in, wheeling the statue between them on a reinforced trolly. Despite the hours she'd spent analyzing every detail, a macabre thrill licked through Emily's chest as the Hound passed her by. There was definitely something unsettling about it—an undeniable presence, as if it would come alive and move at any moment. Yet Emily's gaze moved beyond it to the man walking in just behind them.

Rob Holloway.

Bell's head conservationist moved with muted precision, his crisp white dress shirt immaculately pressed beneath a pair of dark braces that pulled taut against his lean frame. His hair, dark and neatly combed, framed his expression—reserved yet analytical, a man accustomed to control. Which meant the chaos unfolding before them—the volatility of Simon Reed, the mounting stakes—was probably sending his OCD into overdrive.

Yet, he said nothing. He simply nodded once at Jared, at Emily, then turned his attention to the statue.

Simon Reed approached the Hound with caution, though tension still showed beneath his movements. His fingers flexed at his sides, a reflex rather than intention—an unconscious urge to touch, to confirm.

"Step back, Mr. Reed."

Jared's voice cut through the space—low, sharp. Not raised, but enough to turn heads.

One of the guards adjusted his stance, subtle but ready.

Reed exhaled, leveling Jared with a look. "I'm not going to damage it."

"You're not going to touch it at all," Jared replied, firm.

The lawyer leaned in, murmuring something close to Reed's ear. He muttered a curse under his breath before lifting both hands in surrender. "Fine. But I need a closer look."

Emily glanced at Jared, waiting for his reaction. He said nothing, but the muscle in his jaw ticked.

She gave the smallest nod.

Reed crouched beside the Hound's left flank, shifting his weight as he flicked on his phone's torch. He passed the beam slowly over the statue's foundation, brow furrowing as he scanned every detail, magnifying the lens with his fingers to sharpen the focus.

Like most animalistic statues in motion, the Hound was fixed to a thick bronze plate made for counterbalance and securing to other surfaces—like slabs of marble.

Emily thought back to the four rusted holes on the block at the Channings' and rubbed her palm absently. Crouching beside Reed, she angled her own torchlight over the creature. "What exactly are we looking for?"

Reed pressed his lips together, adjusting the angle of his phone as he studied a thin space—a sliver of a gap just wide enough to conceal something—between the beast's massive rear paw and the plate it was screwed to.

"That," he muttered, tilting his screen.

At first, it looked like nothing—just a shadow pooling between the pieces of bronze.

Then she saw it. A thin, black line wedged deep within the narrow space. Almost invisible unless the light caught it just right.

Emily straightened slightly. "Rob." Her voice was steady, but her pulse wasn't. "Can you get in there?"

He gave a silent nod and donned a headlamp, flicking on the magnifying lens as he retrieved a set of precision tools from his satchel.

"I'll need a few minutes," he murmured.

The room fell into a hush as he worked. Every movement was deliberate, careful—the refined skill of a man trained in preservation, not excavation. Jared hovered at Emily's side, arms crossed, his body locked with tension.

Seconds ticked by. Then—"Got it," Rob muttered, pulling back.

A thin, black plastic square rested between his gloved fingers. A floppy disk.

Emily felt the air leave her lungs. *Of all the things...*

Reed took a step forward, but the security guard immediately stepped in, blocking his path. "Don't even think about it," he growled.

"Is that the sixth manuscript?" Emily asked aloud.

Reed blinked, as though surprised by the question. "No,"

he said, shaking his head. "You wanted to know what you're dealing with? It's all on there."

The lawyer cleared his throat, adjusting his stance before speaking. "My client asserts that the deceased"—a brief pause—"expressed, through verbal communication, their intention for my client to take ownership of this item."

Something about his hesitation snagged Emily's attention.

She glanced at Jared, who didn't react—but Reed did, shifting his weight slightly, his gaze lingering on the statue just a second too long.

Emily folded her arms. "Unless your client can produce documentation, that's a hard no. Bell's owns the estate. And this"—she nodded to the disk—"is part of it."

Panic laced Simon Reed's features. "Is that true?" he asked the lawyer.

The man nodded and Reed exhaled sharply, frustration clear in the way his fingers curled and flexed.

"I'll have the disk carefully examined," Emily continued. "If there's no legal reason to hold on to it, you'll get it back. Simon, you have my word."

A muscle ticked in Jared's jaw, but he remained silent.

Reed hesitated, his throat bobbing as he swallowed. "Fine," he said at last. But his gaze flicked between them, his voice becoming more urgent. "Just don't drag this out. You're not the only ones looking."

His parting words sent a chill through Emily, especially considering their recent security breach. She turned to Rob, who was still holding the floppy disk between his gloved fingers as if it might detonate at any moment. In a way, she supposed, it could.

"Get that down to Archives. Immediately," she told him.

Rob gave a quick nod, and all but bolted from the room.

Only once they were alone in the room did Emily speak again, her voice barely above a whisper. "What do you think he meant—'we're not the only ones looking'?"

Jared's expression was stoic, but something dark moved in his eyes. "Let's go find out."

As she passed the Hound, her fingers brushed its bronze head. She waited—for a flicker, a flash, some sense of knowing.

But it gave her nothing.

Bell's security was managed by an external company, except for the on-site guards, including Josh Hartley—an old schoolmate of Jared's who had fallen on hard times after a messy divorce.

Jared had pulled a few strings to get Josh the job, knowing he needed stability—not just for himself, but for his baby daughter. Emily hadn't pried, but she knew Jared well enough to recognize his quiet way of looking out for people. It wasn't charity; Jared trusted him, and from what she'd seen, that trust was mutual. If there was a breach, Josh would do everything in his power to help get to the bottom of it.

But Josh hadn't been on duty last night. Bell's guards were primarily stationed during the day to oversee deliveries, manage visitor access, and handle any immediate security threats. After hours, the building relied on a combination of electronic security measures—access logs, motion sensors, and surveillance cameras—monitored remotely by the external company. Unless an active alarm was triggered, such as forced entry or unauthorized access to restricted areas, they wouldn't immediately intervene.

But after Jared's call, the security team had been running logs and scanning footage to determine not only who the intruder was, but how they had gained access. Josh and the other guards had also started questioning all staff who had been in the building during the evening, focusing on those who couldn't be accounted for at any time.

The thought of them reviewing the elevator footage had sent Emily into a panic, but Jared had assured her the company was discreet—and, more importantly, that the cameras leading to the loft fed directly to him alone, ensuring their privacy.

He'd already checked the footage from last night, confirming that the loft had remained secure. Now, more than ever, it was a stark reminder that she ought to start looking for her own apartment.

Josh met them in the hallway, his freshly shaven jaw set like granite. Everything about him, from his closely cropped blond hair to the crisp lines of his navy blue uniform, filled the space with unspoken authority. "You're going to want to see this."

Inside the security office, Jared and Emily sat as Josh laid out the findings.

"The logs flagged something interesting," he said, clicking through the system. "Mia Callaghan's access card was used twice last night—once earlier in the evening, and then again much later."

Mia was an archival research intern, and it wasn't unusual to see her working late at night. Internships were hard to come by in this industry, and having done a few herself, Emily knew what it was like to put in the long hours, to do whatever it took to make an impression.

She was about to say as much when Jared frowned, pointing at the timestamp. The second entry was well after closing—right around the time they'd returned to the loft.

More importantly, there was no record of her exit.

Emily winced. She hoped the young woman hadn't done something foolish.

"Bring her in," Jared said evenly, though his expression was laced with turmoil. Josh nodded and left the room.

"Be gentle with her, Jay. What if she just got spooked by us coming in late and didn't wish to be found here alone?"

Turning to face her, Jared softly touched her cheek. "I love that you see the good in everyone, Em. But she could've just used her card to leave. She didn't need to use the fire stairs. Something else is going on here."

The door opened and Mia stepped inside, followed by Josh. He pulled out his chair, gesturing for her to sit, and then stood guarding the door. Emily felt sorry for the poor girl, who looked absolutely terrified—her wide eyes nervously darting between Jared and Josh.

"Mia, it's come to our attention that your access card was potentially used to facilitate yesterday's security breach," Jared told her. "Since you didn't report the card as stolen, and then used it this morning, I believe you're already aware of this?"

Mia hesitated, swallowing hard. "I—I let someone in last night."

Jared didn't react, but Josh stepped forward. "Who?"

Her lower lip trembled. "Ethan," she admitted in a whisper. "Ethan Graves. My boyfriend."

Jared's fingers drummed once against the desk. "And why, exactly, did Ethan need to be here after hours?"

Mia winced. "He just wanted to see the Hound of Blackwood Vale in person. He's a huge fan and just got an internship with Barrow's publisher. He begged me." She looked up desperately. "I thought it was harmless. I just let him in for a minute—just a quick look—he wasn't going to touch it, only take a few photos. But he said it wasn't down in the storeroom. So we left."

Josh brought up the footage, verifying that both the motion sensors and cameras in the storeroom showed only one person, presumably Mia, and nothing suspicious.

"So, you're telling me that isn't you?" he asked her, pointing at the screen.

Mia glanced at the screen and bit her bottom lip, which was already trembling. "No," she whispered. "I arranged for Ethan to wear my hoodie, so it wouldn't raise any alarms."

"And where were you during this time?" Jared asked.

"I waited across the street." She cast him a sheepish glance. "Away from the cameras."

To his credit, Jared's expression didn't change. "Can you explain why your card was used again later that night?"

Mia opened her mouth, then shut it. She seemed genuinely confused.

Josh clicked the security footage onto the screen, fast-forwarding to the breach. And there it was—the same figure slipping out of the stairwell. "That your boyfriend?" he asked.

Mia turned away from the screen, arms wrapped tightly around herself. "Yes, that's him," she said, voice barely above a whisper. "He must've gone back while I was asleep. I swear—I didn't know."

Emily's stomach twisted. The admission ruled out Simon Reed as the intruder, but it didn't make her feel any better. Someone had still been inside the building. While they'd been upstairs. Vulnerable.

Jared dragged a hand down his jaw, the scrape of stubble audible in the cramped room. "Mia," he said, tone flat but firm. "Not only did you let someone into the building after hours without authorization—someone with a direct connection to a client—you did it under false pretenses."

Mia winced. "It wasn't like that. He's my boyfriend. He just... he really admires Barrow. He's kind of obsessed. And when I told him about the Hound—that I had access to it—he got this look. I just wanted to impress him."

Jared arched a brow. "Obsessed is one thing. Sneaking back into a secured facility hours later is another. What exactly does Ethan do at Pendleton?"

Mia hesitated.

Jared's voice sharpened. "Mia."

"He's an editorial assistant," she said finally. "Under one of the senior fiction editors."

A beat of silence followed. Emily could practically hear the implications ticking through Jared's brain.

"And you didn't think to mention that sooner?" he asked, incredulous.

"I didn't know it mattered," she blurted. "He's not high up or anything. It's not like he's in acquisitions."

"No," Jared said tightly, "but he has access. And motive. If Pendleton's sniffing around for Barrow's lost manuscript, Ethan wouldn't need to do much to impress the right people."

"He isn't like that," Mia said. "You're making a mistake. It's just fanboy stuff."

"Fanboys write blog posts and join forums," Jared said coldly. "This was something else."

Emily's gaze flicked to the grainy footage frozen on the screen—Ethan's blurred outline mid-sprint toward the fire exit. "He was looking for something specific," she mused. "And he thought it might still be here."

Jared nodded once, grim. "Which means we need to assume

Pendleton's already aware."

"And that we've just lost our element of surprise," Emily added.

Mia cupped her mouth, looking like she might be sick. "I didn't mean for any of this to happen. I didn't know he was going to come back—"

Jared held up a hand. "This isn't about intent anymore, Mia. It's about exposure."

His voice wasn't cruel—but it wasn't forgiving either.

Mia closed her eyes and began fiddling with the rings stacked on her fingers. Emily dropped her head, giving the girl space and quiet dignity.

"I know you've put in a lot of effort during your time here," Jared said, quieter now, "But this isn't something I can overlook. Bell's reputation is built on discretion and trust. That trust was broken."

A soft, choked sound slipped from Mia's throat. "I wasn't trying to hurt anyone."

"I know," he said, his tone gentler, though resolute. "But intent doesn't erase the consequences. I have to make a call here—not just for the firm, but for our clients. I can't keep you on, Mia. And I'm sorry, but I also can't recommend you to another house, not under the circumstances."

Her shoulders sagged. "So that's it."

"Your internship is terminated, effective immediately. You have until midday to collect your things," he said, more businesslike now. "Josh will take your access card."

Mia hesitated—then pulled the lanyard from around her neck and passed it over without consequence.

Jared didn't say anything else. Because there wasn't anything left to say.

Emily watched the girl leave, a pang of sympathy tightening her chest. Losing her internship could derail everything for Mia. Would she recover from this?

"Don't worry. She'll land on her feet," Jared's voice cut through her thoughts. Standing, he turned to Josh. "Find out everything you can on Ethan Graves. I want to know exactly what Pendleton Press was after."

Josh nodded.

As they stepped out of the security office into the hall, Emily murmured, "We're not the only ones looking."

Jared's expression hardened. "No," he said. "We're not."

8

Late Night Confessions

"The words spilled from his lips like blood from an open wound—slow, inevitable, beyond recall. I had not asked for the truth. God help me, I had not wanted it. But there it lay between us now, dark and festering, and neither of us could look away."

~ The Blight on Blackwood Heath

Emily sat curled on the couch, absently working her thumbs over the knots in Jared's shoulders. He was sitting on the floor in front of her, his back against the couch, legs stretched out in front of him, a half-played game of solitaire forgotten on the coffee table. She could feel the tension in him—the way his muscles resisted under her touch before gradually giving in. It had been a hell of a day.

"Did you hear back from Vikram?" she asked, breaking the silence.

"He couldn't retrieve any data from the disk." Jared didn't sound surprised. "Exposure to the elements, and age, have rendered it unreadable. But he's sending it to a buddy who specializes in forensic recovery. Might take a day or two."

Forensic? The word sent a chill down Emily's spine, a stark reminder that even though Jared hadn't pressed charges against Mia, they were still tangled in something much bigger.

"Do you think Ethan will come back?" she asked.

"I highly doubt it." Jared rolled his head loosely, but his tone left little room for discussion.

Emily studied him, the way he flexed the cards in his hands. He was stewing, and she didn't blame him. The implied intention behind the break-in had shaken both of them.

Shifting her position so her legs were on either side of him, she lifted her hands, pressing down with both thumbs into the knots of tension at the base of his neck. He hissed sharply, but didn't move away.

For a while, they sat in companionable silence as she kneaded the muscles gently, feeling his body relax under her fingers. The room itself was quiet, except for the steady tick of the antique clock shelved among Jared's books.

She scanned the titles as her fingers worked. They were mostly mysteries—entire volumes of Sherlock Holmes and Hercule Poirot. Darker, older leather-bound books stood next to newer editions of detective novels. Emily wondered for a moment if these had been young Jared's favorites, or if they were a more recent acquisition. She caught sight of a couple of battered Hardy Boys volumes tucked into a corner.

Her gaze lingered for a beat longer before she spoke aloud, "So, where are you hiding the Trixie Belden books?"

Jared tensed beneath her fingers. The movement was so slight, she almost missed it. He didn't respond at first, focusing instead on the deck of cards in his hands, shuffling them back and forth with practiced ease.

"The what books?" His voice was flat, a little distant.

"Oh, come on." Emily raised an eyebrow, still massaging his shoulders as she tried to lighten the mood. "It's okay if you're a fan," she said, squeezing his shoulder lightly. "I'm not here to judge."

Jared flicked the deck from one hand to another, his jaw tightening, and his silence spoke volumes. She could feel the tension in his body as it radiated off him, and Emily knew she'd hit a nerve—whether intentionally or not. "Not a fan," he muttered.

Emily tilted her head, narrowing her eyes slightly. At the time, his dig had annoyed her, but now she was just plain curious and wasn't ready to let him off the hook that easily.

"You're obviously familiar with the books," she pressed, her tone playful but insistent. "And you were absolutely right. I do carry a map and flashlight in my purse. It's called a cell phone."

He didn't respond, her playful banter falling as flat as the cards in his hand. She tried again.

"Does your mom have a collection? Or do you harbor a secret passion for reading about retro teenage girl detectives?" She couldn't help the smirk that tugged at the corner of her lips. "You can tell me. I won't tease you for secretly wanting to be Jim."

Jared's fingers slowed over the cards in his hands, and a slight flush crept up his neck. His head fell back into her lap, eyes meeting hers, something guarded and almost apologetic behind his gaze.

He let out a slow breath. "My ex was the fan, not me."

Emily froze for a beat, her fingers stilling against his shoulders.

He sighed as he placed the deck of cards down on the table. "She's a Londoner and was fascinated by New York as a kid. She collected the complete set, and I used to read them to her."

"You read to her out loud?" Emily mused. He already had an expressive voice. But with that accent? She could well understand the appeal. "So, you were her own personal Trixie-obsessed audiobook, huh?"

Jared huffed a laugh under his breath, but there was no humor in it. "Something like that." He paused, then added, "I wouldn't say she was obsessed, but she liked the escape. The puzzles. The idea of everything having a neat little solution." His voice softened, as though he were speaking more to himself than to Emily. "Until it didn't."

"What happened?"

Jared closed his eyes and before long, his hands found her bare calves, gliding warmly along their sides before shifting into a massage of his own. It sent tremors through her entire body, made her breath catch, but she forced herself to keep kneading his shoulders like nothing had changed.

"I was young—straight out of school, living in London, studying at Sotheby's. She was older. Sophisticated. It was fun. I was smitten. She was beautiful, experienced, and she taught me a great deal—not just about sex, but about life, about art. I think I knew, even then, that it wouldn't last. That there was no version of her world where I truly fit. It was more than the age gap. Though she never directly said it, I knew I would never be more than a temporary piece in her life. We lasted a few years before she ended it."

His tone wasn't bitter or nostalgic, but even. Like he'd made peace with it. Yet there was something else beneath his words—something stripped bare in a way that resonated with Emily.

She knew the feeling well. She hadn't lived up to Alex's aspirations, either.

She wanted to ask more, to pry at the edges of whatever he wasn't saying, but she could feel the way he had tensed again, the shift in his breathing. "For what it's worth," she said instead, "I think you're perfect just as you are."

Jared's fingers stilled against her leg.

The moment stretched, charged and uncertain. The weight of their kiss the other night still hung between them, unspoken but not forgotten. After a long beat, Jared shifted, leaning forward to resume his game of solitaire, effectively breaking all contact.

"Careful, Em," he said, his voice distant despite their proximity. "I might just start believing you."

She hesitated for the tiniest second, then pushed off the couch, wanting to steer him away from whatever dark place he was sinking into. "Read to me."

Jared glanced up at her, brows pulling together in mild confusion. "What?"

"I want to weigh in on your audiobook prowess." She smiled. "Will you read to me?"

Jared blinked, clearly caught off guard. Then he huffed a small, surprised laugh. "I hate to break it to you, Em, but I don't want to read another Trixie Belden book for as long as I live."

She smirked. "Good. I'd rather you read me something more your own style."

"Oh yeah? And what exactly is 'my style'?"

"Arsène Lupin." She pulled a volume from the shelf, brandishing it at him.

His brow lifted. "You think I have gentleman thief energy?"

"You do have a penchant for beautiful things. Besides, I figured you'd appreciate a man who always has an escape plan."

For a moment, he said nothing. Then, after a short laugh, he reached up, rubbing a hand over his face. "You might be onto something."

"Come on." She walked over to stand beside him and nudged him with her knee. "Read to me."

Jared didn't move right away. His fingers brushed along her leg again, slower this time. But then he sighed, pushed himself up, and took the worn paperback from her.

Without a word, he stretched out on the couch, one arm tucked behind his head, the other holding the book open. Once Emily had shifted to fit into the space beside him, her head against his shoulder, he began to read.

"It was a strange ending to a voyage that had commenced in a most auspicious manner..."

As his voice filled the room, smooth and low, sleep crept in at the edges of Emily's thoughts. She didn't know if it was the warmth of his body beside hers or the steady rhythm of his voice, but for the first time in days, she felt completely safe.

At some point, exhaustion took over.

She wasn't sure when she drifted off, but when she woke in the early morning light, she found herself still curled against him, her cheek resting on his chest. His breathing was deep and even, one arm wrapped loosely around her waist.

For a long moment, she simply lay there, letting it sink in. The weight of his arm. The rise and fall of his chest beneath her. The way their legs had tangled sometime in the night.

Sleeping together—in the truest sense of the word—felt better than anything had in a long, long time.

9

Stranger Than Fiction

"The first body was found at dawn, with eyes wide in eternal terror. The village whispered of a wraith, of its hunger, and of the spirits that walked unseen among them. But spirits do not leave corpses. Monsters do."

~ The Ghosts of Blackwood Ridge

Now that Mia was gone, Emily planned to spend the next day assisting Vikram in the Archives department. With the auction looming, the absence of Mia's meticulous cataloging left a noticeable gap—but it was her departure itself that unsettled Emily the most.

Mia had spent days digitizing Barrow's manuscripts, scanning each page for the secured online listings before her dismissal. But had that been all she'd done?

Emily couldn't shake the nagging suspicion that she might

have made copies for Ethan. A silent betrayal, one hidden beneath routine tasks and cataloged efficiency. Not that they would hold any real value—Pendleton Press would undoubtedly have their own final editions.

Still, the weight of that possibility pressed at the edges of her thoughts. Loose threads had a way of unraveling at the worst possible moment.

Each of the five manuscripts was stored in a brown manila folder, the pages typewritten on cheap, flimsy paper with a black-and-red inked ribbon, much like the one still coiled inside Barrow's vintage Remington downstairs in the storeroom. As she flipped through the pages of *The Hound of Blackwood Vale*, something caught her eye—a slight imperfection in the text. The letter "e" struck slightly higher than the rest, like a misaligned puzzle piece.

Her pulse quickened. Was it just a flaw of the machine, or something else?

Grabbing the remaining four manuscripts, she flipped through the pages, scanning them with fresh eyes, searching for the same inconsistency.

Barrow's second book, *The Ghosts of Blackwood Ridge*, showed the same raised keystroke until about halfway through, where the "e" fell back into alignment. Perhaps the machine had been serviced, or Victor himself had noticed and fixed the fault, because *The Blight on Blackwood Heath*, the third book, was perfectly aligned from start to finish.

But the last two books, *The Curse of Blackwood Bay* and *The*

Haunting of Blackwood Manor, bore the same telltale flaw. The fifth book, in particular, was riddled with uneven keystrokes, the letters slightly skewed as if the typewriter had been tampered with.

As she flicked through Barrow's last remaining work, a single sheet of notepaper slipped from the stack and fluttered to the floor.

Emily picked it up, heart hammering, hoping it was whatever Barrow had been writing in her vision. The handwriting was rushed, the loops and tails of each letter slanting wildly across the page.

But it wasn't written with a fountain pen.

It wasn't even written in ink.

Her fingers traced the indentations where a pencil had pressed hard against the paper.

Graveisthemanwhowalksamongwolves

A rush of sensation flooded her mind—excitement, trepidation, the metallic scent of lead. And then a flicker of something other.

> *Dainty silver rings glint on unfamiliar fingers.*
> *Fingers that rapidly scan the words on the page,*
> *while the other hand note takes one letter at a time.*

The rings were stacked on nearly every knuckle. Jewelry she had admired just yesterday, covering Mia's shaking hands when she had learned her fate.

Emily jerked back, her breath unsteady, the vision fleeing as quickly as it had arrived.

Forcing herself to focus, she turned back to *The Haunting of Blackwood Manor* and flipped to the first misaligned letter.

"G."

Then "r."

Then "a."

One by one, the misplaced letters lined up with the message on the notepaper.

Her stomach twisted.

"Vik," she said carefully, "is it common for typewriter keys to strike out of alignment?"

Vikram glanced up from his work, frowning. "Fairly common, yeah. Older machines can be particularly quirky, but it's not a flaw, if that's what you're asking. Constant hitting of the platen by the typeslugs will shift off-center over time, but they're fairly easy to put back into place."

"So, does that also mean that someone could deliberately tweak a typewriter to raise certain letters? As a way of leaving a code?"

Vikram's brows lifted in surprise. "It's definitely possible. But it'd take a hell of a lot of effort."

Emily studied the notepaper again, her brain finding spaces between the letters almost immediately.

Grave is the man who walks among wolves.

Her fingers curled around the page. "Indeed."

By the time Jared stuck his head in to drag Emily out to lunch, she had uncovered several more cryptic messages.

Even the hunter fears the howl in the dark.
A door left open is an invitation, not an escape.
Ink dries, but the scent of blood lingers.
Footsteps fade, but something still follows.

She pocketed the scrap of paper, intending to raise her findings with Jared over lunch, but they hadn't even reached the front door when his phone buzzed.

Jared glanced at the screen, then at her. "It's Josh." He pressed the speaker button. "Tell me you've got something."

"I've got more than something," Josh replied. "Ethan Graves is clean, but he has an interesting family connection to Pendleton. Franklin Graves, his great-uncle, was Victor Barrow's editor."

Emily exhaled slowly. "Well, that explains Ethan's obsession with Barrow. Is the uncle still alive?"

"No," Josh said. "Frank died in '98. He was 63."

"Damn, that's young," Emily muttered. "I wonder why he

kept silent all those years."

"I might know the answer to that. Give me a second." There was a brief pause on Josh's end, the faint clicking of keys filtering through the speaker. "I quizzed Ethan on his death, and after a call to his father, confirmed his great-uncle developed early on-set Parkinson's disease and was in a nursing home for several years before his death."

Emily's heart sank. "So, does that mean he was losing his memory?"

"Possibly," Josh answered.

A beat of silence stretched between them, the implication settling in. Jared raised his brows. "Rather poetic, don't you think? Thanks, Josh. Keep an eye on the kid, will you?"

Emily bristled. That "kid" was only a couple years younger than her.

"Got it, boss," Josh answered. "Hey, you still heading out for a surf this arvo? Hayley's at her mom's this weekend."

Jared's gaze slid to Emily, slow and deliberate. "I'll let you know," he said, before thumbing the call closed. "You hungry?"

Whatever sting his earlier comment carried fizzled beneath the weight of that look. During the flight back to Washington after delivering the nutcrackers, Jared had regaled her with tales of Aussie life. She hadn't been prepared to hear that both he and his dad surfed regularly. As a result, her brain had already wandered far past lunch—picturing him cutting through the waves in a snug black wetsuit, muscles flexing, saltwater slicking back that annoyingly perfect hair. She'd seen him in less, sure.

But never in motion.

She bit her bottom lip and grinned up at him. "Famished."

The moment they stepped out onto the street, Emily was hit by a wall of heat and the clashing aromas of half a dozen food joints vying for her attention—sizzling oil, toasted bread, something spiced and smoky wafting through the air. Her stomach growled in protest. Jared was scanning the lunch crowds ahead, but Emily slowed, her fingers brushing the folded notepaper in her skirt pocket.

"Before we eat," she said slowly, "I think I found something. In Barrow's manuscripts."

Jared steered her onto the footpath, joining the queue in front of a Mexican restaurant, his brows lifting. "You think?"

"I was scanning the pages and noticed a few patterns in the typeface. Slight variations in alignment—intentional, I think. Like a code." She handed him the folded scrap of notepaper. "I've found five so far. Well, Mia must have found the first one. That's her handwriting."

He skimmed the lines, his expression sharpening with interest. A low whistle escaped him. "You pulled all this from the manuscripts? What do you think they mean?"

"I don't know yet. I wasn't even sure it meant anything," she admitted. "Until I found the second one. Then the third."

"Vik knows?"

"Not yet," she said, watching him closely. "I wanted to run it by you first."

Jared glanced at her sideways, eyes gleaming with something

between admiration and amusement. "And you think you're nothing like Trixie Belden."

She smiled, a little proud now. "Thought I'd at least earn my lunch."

He ushered her inside the restaurant and leaned in, close enough that his voice felt like a secret. "You're doing a hell of a lot more than that, Em." A beat passed—long enough for something unspoken to settle between them. "Come on," he said, nodding toward the menu. "We'll grab something quick and take it back to the office. You can show me everything."

When they arrived back at the Bell's archives, Vikram was seated at his desk, a pile of papers scattered around him, his fingers flying over the keyboard as he worked. He glanced up as they entered, raising an eyebrow at the takeout bags in Jared's hand.

"Lunch?" Vikram asked with a grin, his tone suggesting he didn't really need an answer.

"Yeah," Jared said, sitting at the table and setting the food down. "But we've got more important things to talk about first." He turned to Emily. "Why don't you tell Vik what you found?"

Emily looked between them, buoyed by Jared's confidence. "Barrow left messages hidden within his last couple of manuscripts. I think he knew something or someone was closing in on him." She hesitated, glancing at Jared, before continuing. "They're cryptic, but they're definitely in there."

Vikram's eyes narrowed in thought, his hands resting behind

his head. "Messages? In the text itself?"

Emily nodded. "Misaligned type. Seemingly random letters, but when you string them together, you get entire phrases. All pointing to something. And I think it's connected to Pendleton Press."

Jared's eyes flicked to hers. "The only person who would've read those drafts was Franklin Graves. You think he was trying to tell him something?"

Emily chewed her lip, a growing sense of unease threading through her chest. "I don't think he knew who to trust. But he was obviously leaving a trail. And Mia was the one who spotted it."

Vikram let out a low whistle. "That's—damn. Okay, we need to comb those manuscripts for anything that feels a little off. Misalignments, misspelled words, marginal notes, anything." He gestured to the takeout bags. "But first, we eat."

Jared passed Emily her fish taco, their hands brushing longer than was necessary, his eyes meeting hers constantly over the top of his vegetarian burrito bowl.

She raised a brow. "When did you give up eating meat?"

"I haven't given it up." Jared gave a casual shrug. "A lighter meal means better balance. If I'm surfing later, I don't want to feel weighed down."

Again, her thoughts drifted to where they shouldn't. Jared cutting through the waves with ease, shifting his weight without thought, like gravity had nothing on him. So, when an incoming email chimed on Vik's computer, she welcomed the interruption.

"That was quick," Vic muttered through a mouthful of food. "Data retrieval's come through."

Emily's pulse quickened. She had almost given up hope that anything salvageable would come from the damaged disk. Beside her, Jared abandoned his lunch and crossed to the screen.

"Let's see what we've got."

A few clicks and a flood of files filled the screen. Vik sorted them by type—editorial notes, typed letters, and internal Pendleton Press memos.

"Looks like you were right, Emily," Vik said, opening the files one by one across three screens. "You should see this."

She went to Jared's side and leaned in, her eyes darting across the text.

The first document—a memo between Derek Caldwell and Wesley Cartwright—was chilling in its simplicity:

Barrow remains resistant. If he refuses to complete the manuscript, we will proceed without him. Graves needs to get him in line.

She inhaled sharply. "Graves. They're talking about Ethan's great-uncle Franklin, right?"

Jared gave a grim nod. "Looks like he was tasked with controlling Barrow."

Grave is the man who walks among wolves.

Emily frowned, Barrow's cryptic message gnawing at her. "Maybe. But look at this."

She pointed to another document that Vik had just pulled

up—a compilation of revision notes for *The Haunting of Blackwood Manor*. The comments seemed innocuous at first, standard edits and suggestions, but one line stood out among the others.

There are too many hands on this now. If you still know what's real, trust it.

Her skin prickled. "That doesn't sound like someone trying to 'get him in line.'"

Vikram's fingers flew over the keyboard, pulling up more documents. "Wait... there's more." He opened a letter addressed to Victor Barrow. It was brief and cryptic, yet it told them everything they needed to know.

The wolves are prowling. You're not imagining any of it. Stay silent. Trust no one but me.

It was signed with two simple letters: F.G.

Unlike the other letters written by Graves, there was no complimentary close. No signature with his name. No *Senior Editor, Pendleton Press*.

Emily felt her breath hitch. "He wasn't working against Barrow. He was trying to protect him."

Returning to the table, Emily picked up *The Haunting of Blackwood Manor*, the aged paper crinkling under her fingertips as she flipped through the editorial notes, presumably written by Ethan's great-uncle. After Barrow's cryptic message of ***Even the hunter fears the howl in the dark***, a comment penned in faded red ink appeared in the margin, hinting at a deeper meaning. She read it out loud.

"Might be stronger if the protagonist doubts his own reality—if he sees wolves where there are none."

Her pulse kicked up. She grabbed another page and found more.

"Reads like a shadow you didn't invite. Are you sure it belongs in this room?"

She backtracked the manuscript to find this one appeared after Barrow's message: **A door left open is an invitation, not an escape**. The hairs on the back of her neck stood up. When read together, the inference was clear: *Someone inserted this. You didn't write it.*

"These aren't just revision suggestions," she exclaimed. "They're messages for Victor."

While Graves's notes were scattered throughout all five manuscript drafts—sometimes in the margins, sometimes slipped into suggested line rewrites—on the surface, they appeared to be standard editorial feedback and could very well be nothing more. But, if Barrow knew what to look for...

"I get that Barrow wrote horror, but why were they *both* being so cryptic? If Graves knew what was happening at Pendleton, why not just warn Barrow outright?" Vikram asked.

"Because he couldn't," Jared said, his tone dark. "Pendleton would've had him on a tight leash."

Emily put down the manuscript. "Michael should also be across this. He can cross-check each draft with the final product. That way, we can see what was altered post-edit."

"Good idea." Jared pulled out his phone and dialed his rare

books specialist. "Mike, it's Jared. You need to get down to Vik's office now. And bring Barrow's novels."

"Bloody hell," Vikram murmured. "Look at this." He brought up another memo, this time from Cartwright to Caldwell.

CONFIDENTIAL Internal Memo—Blackwood Series Development
We are approaching the final stage. Barrow's deterioration is progressing as expected, ensuring the fifth book carries the raw, unfiltered tone necessary to cement his legacy. The work now carries an unnerving authenticity that cannot be replicated through conventional editorial refinement.
The manuscript must be completed before intervention, as stabilization at this stage would jeopardize its integrity. Once delivered, we proceed as planned.

"Barrow wasn't losing his mind," Emily breathed. "He was being pushed over the edge."

A long silence stretched between them as the realization sank in.

Emily could picture it so clearly: a brilliant, reclusive writer questioning his own reality, manipulated at every turn by a company that saw him as nothing more than a commodity. And in the middle of it all, one man—Franklin Graves—trying to send warnings that Barrow probably couldn't even trust himself to believe.

Jared's hands dropped to his hips, jaw clenched. "And it worked," he said, voice low with disgust. "They got exactly what they wanted. The myth. The masterpiece. The martyr."

"But if Frank thought Pendleton were onto them," Emily exhaled thoughtfully. "What happened to him?"

Vikram spun back to his computer. "I think I know." He clicked open the final dated file—a company memo, cold and clinical in its wording.

Effective immediately, Franklin Graves is no longer with Pendleton Press. His role will be reassigned.

No explanation. No follow-up. Just a swift and silent removal.

Emily stared at the screen, her heart pounding. Graves had tried to warn Barrow. He had left behind breadcrumbs, hidden messages. But it hadn't been enough. She swallowed, her fish taco sitting queasily in her belly. "He got too close."

Jared nodded, jaw tight. "And they silenced him."

A chill ran through her. "We need to show this to Simon Reed."

"And then?" Jared's gaze met hers, steady and unyielding.

Emily clenched her jaw. "Then we make damn sure Pendleton Press doesn't get away with it."

10

A Personal Stake

*"The hound's cry echoed through the valley,
a mournful wail that sent a shiver through
the bones of the land itself. It did not hunt
for sport, nor for vengeance—its purpose
was older, bound in blood and shadow,
and it would not rest until its duty was
fulfilled."*

~ The Hound of Blackwood Vale

Emily rang Simon Reed, and he agreed to meet with them the following morning at ten.

The rest of the afternoon was spent crammed in Vikram's office, the manuscripts spread across the table like a crime scene. Pages layered with red-ink annotations and printed internal memos told a story more disturbing than any of them had expected.

And Graves, despite his loyalty, had been caught in the

middle. Whether complicit or coerced, he'd tried to leave a trail—one he must have hoped Barrow would understand.

When Michael cross-checked the draft manuscript against the published edition of *The Haunting of Blackwood Manor*, the discrepancy was undeniable. Whole passages had been rewritten, twisted into something darker, more fractured. The final version bore no co-writing credits, yet Barrow's voice had been manipulated, and by someone else's hand.

Though visibly rattled by the discovery, Michael couldn't hide his awe. His expressions veered wildly between fascination and horror, punctuated by theatrical gasps that reminded Emily—most definitely—of her Uncle Pete. He leaned over the table, tracing a finger over the manuscript just above one of the coded annotations.

"Incredible," he breathed. "It's like editorial espionage. These aren't just margin notes—this is an entire conversation hidden in plain sight. Between the lines. Between the *versions*."

Then, with a sharp shake of his head, the awe vanished from Michael's face. "This isn't just literary sleight of hand—this is evidence. Possibly criminal. If Pendleton gets even a whiff of what we've uncovered..." He looked at Jared. "You can't let these manuscripts go under the hammer next week. That auction needs to be stopped."

"Like hell it does," Jared muttered, already pulling out his phone. "We'll attach a caveat. Stop the sale from clearing without a legal review. We've already got digital copies, backups—everything. But the auction goes ahead. I'm settling it with Jess now."

Emily glanced at Vikram, who gave a terse nod.

"This isn't about the revenue," Jared said with a direct look at her. "It's about not letting Pendleton know we're on to them. It's our turn to 'proceed as planned'." He was already halfway out the door, phone pressed to his ear.

Michael shook his head. "I hope Jess knows what she's doing."

"She's been around forever, man, don't stress," Vik said with a grin.

Emily frowned. "I don't think I've met her yet. Who is she?"

Michael waved a vague hand and began collecting the paperbacks. "She handles all our legals. Pretty sharp. But this isn't a simple contract or compliance matter. I don't think we've come across something like this before." With a half-hearted raise of his hand, he opened the door, leaving Emily and Vikram alone.

"Are you going to finish that?"

Emily turned to find Vik eyeing the remains of her fish taco. Her appetite had long since vanished—crushed under the weight of everything they'd just uncovered. She nudged it toward him. "Be my guest."

He snatched it off the table with zero hesitation and a muffled "Thanks," already halfway through his first bite.

"You ever wonder," she asked softly, "if maybe we shouldn't be the ones telling this story?"

It was the first time she'd doubted her purpose since laying her hands on the statue of the Hound of Blackwood Vale. Couldn't drown the thought that it was all her doing. Not her fault, obviously, but she'd been the one to unearth it all. To chase Simon Reed down like a hellhound on his trail, and now there was no stopping what she'd started.

Vik paused mid-chew. "If not us, then who? At least we're trying to do the right thing."

Emily didn't respond. She just gave a nod that wasn't really a nod and stood to clear the table.

"Leave it," Vikram said, removing the manila folders from her hand. "I'll do this. Go home. Put your feet up. Kick that jetlag in the butt."

She gave him a small smile. "Thanks Vik. Call me if I can help with anything, okay?"

"You know I won't."

"Yeah, but still—" She was going to add: "You know where I live" until she realized that maybe the rest of the Bell's staff weren't aware that she was holing up in Jared's loft. Except for Sofia, of course. Emily stopped by her desk on the way up, noting Jared's empty office. Sofia told her he had left for the afternoon but wasn't sharing any details.

Taking Vik's advice, she went upstairs and ran a warm bath, scrolling through local apartment listings while she waited for the tub to fill. She bookmarked a few places, keen for Jared's opinion on location and value for money.

But as the sun dipped, and the shadows lengthened across the loft, the silence began to press in. Emily stood barefoot in the kitchen, the kettle boiling behind her, waiting for a sound—*any* sound—that might signal Jared had come home. The hours had slipped by in pieces: her hands on autopilot as she tidied the living room, filled a wine glass, folded the same throw blanket three times. It wasn't the silence that unnerved her. It was what her mind filled it with.

Her thumb traced the rim of the glass. Where he was shouldn't matter. It *didn't* matter. Except that it did. She put the wine down and stared at the candle she'd lit earlier. The one that sat on a tray at the end of the counter with a few other artfully arranged knick-knacks. The aroma was heavenly—lemon balm, citrus and something earthy. The vase that contained it was equally beautiful—swirled carnival glass in molten streaks of red, orange and white. Only it didn't *quite* fit with Jared's décor.

The thought snuck in before she could stop it—uninvited, unwanted, but not entirely irrational. She picked it up. It was heavier than she expected, colder too. But as the cool surface gradually gave way to the warmth of her palms, she closed her eyes and opened her mind.

Darkness blooms behind her lids, before shuttering to bright sunlight and colorful, fluttering canvas flags—a street market, most likely somewhere in Southern Europe. The melodic banter of several vendors lilts through the air, and then—her breath catches—a familiar Australian accent.

Jared appears—youthful, carefree, his arm draped around a slender woman with sleek bobbed hair and impeccable style. The woman volleys off flawless Italian to the stallholder before picking up the candle. Jared takes it from her with a smile.

The scene shifts—effortlessly, cruelly—to a shadowed bedroom, where French doors are thrown wide to the night. Jared reclines on rumpled sheets, bronzed and bare-chested, his arm now curved protectively around the same woman's naked shoulders. A book grasped in the other hand, his voice low and intimate. He is reading. To her. His ex.

In bed.

Emily's eyes flew open, heart skittering. She set the vase down too firmly, swapped it for her glass, but the wine tasted off now—bitter with something she didn't want to examine too closely. Rising from the couch, she began pacing the kitchen. Lucy lifted her head from the floor with a soft whine, ears pricked.

"It's my own fault," Emily murmured to the dog. "I shouldn't have pried into his personal life."

She hadn't let herself do that in years. It left a bitter tang in her chest—guilt, and something dangerously close to jealousy.

She fed Lucy distractedly, trying not to think about the woman Jared used to love. Might still love, if he'd kept something sentimental from their time together.

She wondered if he ever thought about her when he lit the candle.

She knew she would.

Wondering if he'd notice if she moved it out of sight, she was mid-step across the kitchen when the elevator groaned to life. Lucy looked up from her dinner and wagged her tail, but went straight back to eating. Emily stood stock still, her pulse jumping.

Jared flung the door wide and stepped inside, looking like he'd weathered a tempest—dripping seawater and streaked with sand, his board tucked under one arm, hair wet and curling at the ends. He smelled of the sea—of salt, sweat, and the storm he hadn't been able to outrun.

She didn't ask where he'd been. She didn't need to. Instead, she asked if he was okay.

He gave a slow nod. "Yeah. Just needed to clear my head."

"I know the feeling," she said, offering a wry smile. "I drowned in a sea of bubbles for an hour."

Jared's gaze dropped to the wineglass beside her, one brow lifting in mild amusement.

"Not champagne," she said quickly. "I had a bath, and probably left underwear on the floor now that I think of it, so—ignore that."

His mouth twitched, but he said nothing.

"I can throw something together for dinner while you shower, if you're hungry." She didn't even look up as she said it, already shifting toward the fridge like the answer was obvious.

She didn't notice Jared still standing there until she turned around. It wasn't like he was weighing the offer, but like it had caught him completely off guard.

She frowned slightly. "Or not."

It was a small act. Something she could do to repay him for the kindness of letting her stay. And that would take her mind away from her vision and the guilt that had followed it.

He gave a slow nod. "Yeah. That'd be nice."

Busying herself while Jared disappeared down the hall, Emily gathered ingredients for chili. It had always been her comfort food growing up, and homesickness tugged at her just enough to crave it.

Jared clearly liked to cook—his pantry was more stocked than she'd expected for a bachelor. No beans, but she found canned tomatoes, onions, a lone bell pepper, and just enough ground beef to make it work. He even had everything for her dad's homemade spice mix.

As she pulled pots and pans from the cabinet beneath the stove, Lucy watched—ears pricked, tail thumping with anticipation.

Emily caved, tossing her a small lump of beef. Lucy caught it midair, and Emily couldn't help but smile.

Soon, the scent of browning meat and warm spices filled the loft, anchoring her in something solid, the motions of cooking easing the tightness in her chest. She didn't want to think anymore about the candle or the vision. Didn't want to dwell on the fact that she'd stepped into Jared's past without permission.

Tonight, she just wanted to be here. With him. Looking ahead, not behind.

By the time he reappeared, fresh from the shower and dressed in a clean T-shirt and sleep pants, she was scooping chili into stoneware bowls, a sprinkle of cheese on top and warmed tortillas on the side in place of cornbread.

Jared leaned over the pot and gave an exaggerated sniff. "I thought you were Washingtonian, not Texan."

She smirked. "That's true. And this would be sacrilege in Texas—you don't have the right peppers for proper mesquite heat."

He chuckled under his breath and took a seat, watching her with warm eyes as she handed him a bowl and joined him at the counter. He topped up her glass of wine before fetching a beer from the fridge and settling onto the stool beside her.

"This smells amazing, Em. Thank you."

She gave him a shy smile. "It's my dad's signature dish. Hope I've done it justice."

He scooped a large spoonful into his mouth, his eyes fluttering closed in pleasure as he swallowed. "It's good. Really good."

They ate quietly for a while, the silence not uncomfortable, but thick with thought. Lucy let out a groan and sprawled under the coffee table.

Emily pushed her spoon through the chili, then set it down again.

"I found a couple of furnished apartments while I was soaking earlier," she said, keeping her tone light. "Thought I might get your opinion. One of them is within walking distance, historic building, old-world furnishings, and really spacious. The other is light and bright. It's in Pyrmont, but... I don't know. It felt more like me."

Jared didn't respond at first. Just kept his eyes on his bowl, slowly working through the last of his meal. Worried she'd said the wrong thing, Emily opened her mouth to backtrack—but hesitated. She hadn't meant to imply his home wasn't somewhere she wanted to stay. Still, something in Jared's posture shifted—so slight it might've gone unnoticed, but she caught it. Not quite tension, but a tightening—like a door closing softly somewhere inside him. He wasn't annoyed. Just... holding something in reserve.

Emily reached for her wine, letting the sip fill the silence she didn't quite know how to breach. She didn't want to push. Didn't want to misread the moment—or overstay her welcome.

Not after what she'd seen—Jared, bare-chested and content—reading by candlelight to someone in a bed that wasn't hers. And that same candle—the one he'd bought for his sophisticated ex—now sat on his kitchen counter.

She told herself it didn't mean anything. And it probably didn't.

Yet it nudged something loose in her. Urged her to move

forward.

"Let me know when you want to see them," he said. "I'll come with you." His voice was soft, the words landing carefully. Rehearsed. Like he wasn't sure how to say what he really meant.

She smiled. "That would be great. Thanks."

They moved through the cleanup in easy silence at first—until Emily nudged him with her elbow as he reached for a plate, a challenge in her smirk. Jared answered with a subtle bump of his own, his grin widening when she swatted him away with the dish towel.

Their playful exchanges faded into a steady rhythm, their movements syncing in a way that required no words.

It felt strangely normal—too normal. Like they'd done it a hundred times before. Like this was their regular Thursday. And maybe that was what scared her most—not what she'd seen in that flicker of his past, but how quickly she could imagine fitting into his present.

He grabbed a dish towel and wiped the counter, his movements unhurried.

"About the apartments," she said carefully. "I wasn't saying I want to move out right now. I just... I don't want to assume."

He looked at her then. Really looked. And something behind his expression almost cracked—but didn't.

"You can assume," he said.

Three words. Steady. Soft. Loaded.

She wanted to ask what he meant. If it meant *stay*. If it meant something more. But she didn't. Instead, she nodded, slow. Let the weight of the moment sit between them.

And in the quiet that followed, something tender and unmistakable unfolded—like the beginning of a promise neither of them was quite ready to speak aloud.

Because it wasn't just the past that refused to stay buried.

It was everything they were becoming.

Emily hadn't slept well, her thoughts spiraling and keeping her awake into the wee hours. When she finally stepped into the conference room with minutes to spare ahead of Simon Reed, she froze.

Jared was already seated at the far end of the table, shoulders tense, expression tight. Beside him, elegant and composed, sat a woman in tailored black, an iPad resting on her elegantly crossed legs like it belonged there. Her sleek bob was sculpted with precision, her blood-red lips a statement of intent. She carried herself with the kind of poise sharpened by experience—not dulled by time.

Recognition slammed into Emily like a wave. She didn't need an introduction.

Oblivious, Jared stood anyway. "Emily Sloane, this is Jessica Cotillard," he said, his voice smooth but strained. "Jess is our compliance lawyer and has already been briefed." He cleared his throat.

Emily hesitated for a beat too long before extending her hand. "Of course. Nice to meet you." Her fingers met Jess's in a cool, professional shake, careful not to brush any jewelry that might give her a glimpse into this woman's past.

Sofia opened the conference room door, stepping aside as Simon Reed entered. He gave a small, tight nod to the room, followed by his lawyer—who said nothing as he took a seat beside his client, eyes sweeping the room.

As they all settled, Jared shifted in his seat, his jaw clenched.

Emily sat stiffly beside Vikram, heart thudding in her chest. Jared's position beside Jess was intensely distracting; overshadowed by their unshared past.

Vik leaned closer to her, his voice barely a whisper. "Emily. Get your head in the game."

She nodded, blinking hard. Pulled herself upright.

On his laptop, Vikram pulled up the decrypted contents of the floppy disk. The room's lighting dimmed in readiness as emails and memos filled the projected screen—dated, damning. There were editorial notes from Franklin Graves, internal memos bearing Pendleton's letterhead, plus the added scanned manuscript pages detailing the clandestine correspondence between Barrow and his editor that Emily herself had uncovered.

Finally, Reed broke the silence. His voice was quieter than she expected. "You really got it all."

Jared met Simon's gaze, unflinching. "There's a lot of damning evidence in this room, enough to burn reputations to the ground," he said, his voice low and controlled. "So before any of this goes public, I need to know exactly what your role was. You said you'd give us answers—now's the time. Because without the truth, we don't have the whole story. And we're not telling it half-finished."

Jess leaned forward, her voice cool as she addressed Reed's lawyer. "Before we proceed, we need to establish safeguards—for Bell's, for your client, and for the estate—given the nature of the material we've recovered."

She produced a set of documents and laid them on the table. "These are standard non-disclosure agreements. Everyone in this room will need to sign one before any specifics are discussed."

Reed's lawyer adjusted his glasses and flipped through the stack. "Understood." He passed a copy to Reed. "This is expected. You're protected."

But Reed didn't pick up the pen. His gaze remained locked on the screen containing the digitized contents of the disk.

"I'm not here to fight you on this," he said quietly. "I just want the record straight. I want it known what Graves was doing—what he was made to do. I inherited the fifth book's edit, but I knew something was off. Barrow thought as much. He was losing his grip, and now I understand why."

Emily watched him carefully. "So why show up now?"

"For the same reason you are. The timing. Barrow might have fallen out of favor, but the Blackwood anniversary has changed all that. And because I didn't stop it," Reed said, voice tight. "I saw the cracks. I ignored them. And I won't let Pendleton bury this too."

Jared exchanged a glance with Jess, then nodded once. "Then let's make sure they don't."

After they all signed the NDA, Reed sat back, the lines around his mouth deepening with something like shame.

"Pendleton approached me just after Barrow turned in the fifth manuscript. Said he needed *support*." He glanced at Jess, then Jared. "I assumed they meant editorial. Structural help. Maybe a little ghost-polishing. Happens all the time—authors burn out, deadlines loom."

Emily stayed silent, watching how tightly his hands knotted in his lap.

"But it became clear pretty quickly," Reed went on, voice tightening, "they didn't mean support. They meant control. Under the radar. Uncredited."

He rubbed a hand over the back of his neck.

"At first it was small things that wouldn't raise any red flags—cleaning up his prose, fixing transitions, things his editor should have been doing. I didn't know at the time that Graves had been stood down until they started sending me entire chapters to be rewritten.

"That was when I started noticing a pattern. The revisions weren't just about tightening his writing—they were changing it. The tone, the phrasing, even the way his ideas unfolded. It was subtle at first, almost seamless, but the more I worked on them, the more I realized I wasn't just polishing his words. I was

135

shaping them.

"They'd brought me in to make the transition seem natural—to keep his style intact while quietly steering the narrative where they wanted it. At first, Barrow didn't question it. Then he did. He started second-guessing everything, asking for drafts he'd already signed off on, scrutinizing passages like they weren't his own—even when I hadn't touched them.

"Sometimes he refused to approve a chapter until it had passed through my hands—not because he trusted me, but because he didn't trust himself. Like he believed someone else had written his book—and worse, that he couldn't prove it."

A heavy silence fell over the room.

"They framed it as preservation," Reed said bitterly. "That we were doing the hard thing for the right reasons." He looked down, voice soft. "I wanted to believe that. But I wasn't simply ghostwriting." His gaze lifted to Emily, raw and unguarded. "I was gaslighting him."

Jared leaned forward, elbows on his knees, voice low. "Why would you manipulate him like that?"

Reed exhaled sharply, rubbing his hands over his face, as if trying to wipe away years of regret. "You think I wanted to?"

He looked up then, gaze raw and unguarded. "Picture this—your wife has a rare blood disorder. Degenerative. Progressive. You try everything. Stem cell therapy. Clinical trials. Transfusions every six weeks. None of it is covered by insurance. Not a damn thing."

His voice tightened. "Then someone offers you bonuses,

under-the-table payments, a ghostwriting contract wrapped in NDAs so tight it feels like..." He swallowed hard, as if fighting back tears. "It feels like you're selling your own soul to save her body."

Emily's heart sank. "You felt like you had no choice."

"I didn't have a choice," Reed snapped, then caught himself, jaw tightening. "You've got to understand, I didn't change Barrow's words secretly. I was following directives. For Christ's sake, I was twenty-four years old, and my wife was *dying*. Tell me you wouldn't have done the same."

He sucked in a breath, his hands curling into fists on the table, before reaching for the water carafe. The room remained still and silent, while he poured himself a glass and drank it with shaking fingers.

"I didn't stay with Pendleton solely for the money. It wasn't just about Clare." His voice dropped, rough and unsteady. "I stayed for Barrow, too. When it got bad. When he refused to sleep and started pacing the halls like a man waiting for something to find him." His gaze flickered, haunted. "He believed the Hound was real."

Emily stilled, but Jared leaned forward, the tension in the room thickening. "What do you mean—real?"

Reed's throat bobbed. "That it was more than just fiction. He was certain of it. Told me he could feel it breathing in his room, watching him from the dark corners. There were nights he wouldn't turn his back to the windows."

Michael narrowed his eyes. "And you just went along with

it?"

"I told myself I was there to help him—to keep things from spiraling out of control. But the truth?" Reed hesitated, then let out a bitter laugh. "The truth is, I was afraid to leave."

Jared leaned forward, eyes sharp. "Afraid of what?"

Reed finally met his gaze, and for the first time, there was no bitterness—only resignation. "That if I left, it would take him. And I would lose them both."

Emily's heart clenched. "So you kept working."

"So I kept working." Reed's voice barely rose above a whisper. He stared at the edge of the table for a moment, lost in something far away. "Clare died eight years ago," he said finally, his voice softer now. "And now I've got Briony to look out for—she's nineteen, studying literature of all things. God help me." A faint, bitter smile. "She thinks I'm some noble old workhorse who stayed out of the spotlight because I cared more about the words than the glory."

"She doesn't know." Jared's voice was quiet.

Reed shook his head, weariness etched into every line of his face. "Pendleton has held this over my head for decades. They threatened to leak emails, altered drafts—things they'd twisted to make it look like I was trying to steal Victor's legacy." He paused, running a hand over his short hair. "They painted me as resentful, envious, desperate. That if anything leaked, the press would eat it up—frame me as the bitter ghostwriter who wanted to replace a legend."

He took off his watch. Flipped it over to read the words

inscribed on the back, before slipping it back on with a sigh. "I'm so done with hiding in the shadows. I'm ready to stand in the spotlight, but they won't strike the sixth *Blackwood* book from the contract. They shoot down every request, every demand, claiming it's still part of the franchise, even though I wrote it after Barrow's death. I can't win."

Jess pinned Reed's lawyer with her shrewd gaze. "Surely the original contract had reversion clauses and conditions?"

"There was no automatic reversion of rights upon Victor Barrow's passing."

The man flipped through his notes, handing her a copy of what was presumably Simon Reed's publication contract.

"Barrow's original contract explicitly stated that Pendleton retained rights until the full series was completed, meaning that the sixth book—regardless of who wrote it—still falls under their control. Further to that, my client was contractually bound to continue writing under Barrow's name, meaning Pendleton could claim that the work remains part of the franchise, even posthumously."

"Bastards," murmured Vik.

"Wait a minute." Emily's brain was still trying to catch up. "Did you say that you've already written the book? That it's not just a rumor—there really is a sixth manuscript?"

Reed nodded, exhaling shakily. "It's done. I've been sitting on it for years." His voice was raw, edged with something brittle. "Pendleton made it clear that if I tried to ever publish it myself, they'd destroy me. They said if Briony ever looked up my name, all she'd find was scandal. Disgrace. That she'd grow up in the shadow of my guilt."

Emily's chest tightened. She flicked a glance at Jared—his expression had shifted, not with pity, but with something closer to understanding.

Reed let out a slow breath, like he was forcing himself to settle before saying more. "I told myself I could live with Victor's death. That I could walk away, having done all I could. But the longer I stayed silent, the more it ate at me."

His fingers tapped absently against the table, the movement restless, distracted. "I dug around, but Pendleton covered their tracks well. Then one day, I get a call from a guy. He tells me Barrow's deterioration, the book contracts, the pressure—it's all there if you know where to look."

Emily didn't press him. Pushing wouldn't gain his trust—and right now, she needed that more than a confrontation. But curiosity tugged at her too, sharp and unresolved.

Because of all the fragments the Hound had shown her, this part—the moment the disk was hidden—was just... absent.

And that absence nagged at her, louder now than ever.

"It was Franklin Graves, wasn't it?" she said. "The guy."

Jess straightened slightly, tapping a note on her iPad. "Victor Barrow's senior editor at Pendleton Press?"

"That's right," Simon confirmed. "Frank reached out to me not long after I started with Pendleton. Said he didn't trust what they were doing. I effectively took his job, but he still wanted to warn me. Said he knew Barrow hadn't written *Blackwood Manor* on his own." Reed gave a mirthless laugh. "I thought he was just bitter at first. Then delusional. Especially when he told me that back in his day, he'd begun keeping company records—letters, contracts, memos, things that he ought to have deleted. Sounded paranoid as hell to me at the time..."

His voice dropped slightly, something heavier settling into his expression.

"Turns out he had a right to be."

Emily's mind spun as she looked over the screen in front of her. Graves's evidence was writ large for everyone to see. Whether he knew he had a neurodegenerative condition at the time or not, that paranoia had led him to protect his intellectual property while he could.

"But why wait so long?" she asked. "If he was already fired, what did he have to lose by keeping silent?"

"You don't understand how desperate Pendleton was. They practically built their name on Barrow's success. By the late 80s, the publishing industry was shifting fast. Big houses were absorbing small ones, and genre fiction—especially horror—was becoming incredibly lucrative. Newer players were dominating shelf space and Pendleton needed Barrow's next book not just for profits, but to prove they still mattered. They were mid-negotiation on a film deal—and needed the series to survive. But by then, Barrow was already declining. He was often confused and resistant. His words were both brilliant and—I don't want to speak ill of the dead—but bloody awful all at the same time. They leaned on Graves to keep him going, claiming it was about legacy and love for the work. Frank genuinely cared for Victor, but he also had his own interests to look out for. He agreed—until he couldn't anymore."

"Because of his own declining mental health."

Simon Reed nodded at Jared. "The disk was his insurance. He wanted me to keep it safe in case something happened to him, but I was already scared. With my wife's condition... I couldn't afford to expose them, or risk keeping evidence at my place." He hesitated, his gaze distant. "That's when I asked myself—what would Victor do? The answer was crystal clear. I'd spent enough long nights with him to know he believed that damn statue was more than just garden decor. More than superstition. I called Frank and convinced him that no one would think to check there, and he said he'd look after it."

Emily let out a breath that felt heavier than it should have.

"I know it sounds ridiculous, but if the truth needed protecting, there was no better guardian than Barrow's Hound."

A hush fell over the room, heavy and thick as dust. Jared flicked a thoughtful glance at Emily, and she nodded. It all made sense now. Franklin Graves must have had someone plant the disk beneath the statue. Someone with no skin in the game—a relative, or a trusted friend—who just went through the motions, not leaving any personal imprint or trace of emotion behind for the statue to absorb.

"And when the auction was announced, you couldn't risk

Pendleton reclaiming the Hound—especially if the disk was still inside. If they found it, the whole truth could disappear before anyone ever knew it existed," Emily said gently.

"I seriously considered coming clean after Clare died and bringing it all to light. My career was in tatters—I'd hit rock bottom. What else did I have to lose? I even attempted to retrieve the disk myself." His eyes flicked to Emily's. "But in the end, I couldn't risk staining Victor's legacy. More than that, I couldn't jeopardize Briony's safety. She's all I have. But the Blackwood anniversary really put a time limit in place. I knew this would be my last chance." He buried his head in his hands. "God, I hate what they've turned me into."

Emily looked at him—really looked at him. Simon Reed wasn't just a man buried by guilt, but a father trying to shield the last precious thing he had left. His shoulders curled inward, like he'd spent too long under the weight of something he'd never meant to carry.

Jared leaned forward, his palm steady as it landed on the table. "Simon. This is your moment. We can help you make it right."

Reed raised glassy eyes. "How?"

Emily stood suddenly, as an idea took hold. Everyone in the room turned to look as her chair scraped across the floor. Unfazed, she met Simon Reed's weary gaze head-on.

"We have the data. We have the narrative. What we don't have is your voice."

II

The Calm Before the Storm

"Fear is a strange thing—it quickens the pulse, sharpens the mind. But the fear I felt in that moment was something else, something deeper. It was the fear of prey when the hunter draws near."

~ The Curse of Blackwood Bay

Emily barely slept. Her mind was still spinning with the excitement of yesterday's epiphany—finally, a way forward for Simon Reed. So, when she spotted Jared attempting to slip out of the loft at dawn for an early morning surf, she caught him at the door. "Mind if I join you?" she asked, her voice brimming with enthusiasm.

Jared paused mid-step, wetsuit half-zipped, keys dangling from his fingers. He gave her a quick once-over, a brow arching at her Washington Huskies hoodie, and the to-go cup of coffee clutched in her hand.

"You want to come *surfing*?"

"I want to watch *you* surf," she corrected, already tugging on her sneakers. "After yesterday, I could use the sea air. And so could Lucy."

Since the night of the break-in, Jared hadn't gone back to his parents' place. He'd stayed at the loft—for her peace of mind, mostly—but Lucy had stuck close too, like she'd appointed herself Emily's shadow. At the sound of her name, the big black dog bounded over the couch and landed at Emily's feet, ears up and tail sweeping the floor. Jared huffed a laugh, then pulled the door open wider. "Alright then. Let's go."

The beach was anything but sleepy when they arrived. Dog walkers and joggers already populated the shoreline, and past the breaking waves, surfers dotted the deep blue water. A soft haze clung to the horizon, the sky painted in streaks of pink and apricot. It was the kind of morning that made everything seem like it might just turn out okay.

Lucy bolted toward the shore the moment her paws hit the sand, chasing seagulls with abandon. Jared nodded toward the water, where a solitary figure was already paddling out beyond the flags of the patrolled surf area.

"Josh," he said. "Always beats me out here."

Emily followed his gaze out to the swelling whitecaps, then looked back at Jared. "This is how you unwind?"

He offered a faint smile, then zipped the rest of his suit. "It's how I remember I'm small. Helps with perspective."

"Right," she said, brushing windblown hair from her face.

"Just you, the waves, and your existential crises."

He grinned and surprised her with a quick kiss. "Exactly."

Emily slipped off her shoes and wandered down to the water's edge, relishing the feel of the soft sand beneath her feet and the tide nipping at her toes. It was a far cry from the beaches back home in Washington. No stones on the shoreline, no wilderness pressing at her back. She sipped her coffee and soaked in the rising sun, letting the salty air clear her head.

Lucy snapped at the waves a few more times before retreating toward the dunes, coughing up a mouthful of seawater as she went. Emily reached into her pocket, pulled out a rubber ball, and gave it a firm toss down the beach. The dog immediately changed course, her focus switching from foam to fetch without hesitation.

Emily watched her go, a fond smile tugging at her lips. She hadn't expected to grow attached to the giant black hound—but here she was, worried about saltwater intake and hydration like a concerned dog-mom. Lucy bounded back moments later and dropped the ball neatly at Emily's feet, tail wagging, eyes bright.

They settled into a rhythm—throw, chase, return—while the morning sun crept higher in the sky. She peeled off her hoodie and knotted it around her waist, the sunlight highlighting the rich green of the bikini she'd impulsively bought before flying to Australia—emerald against sand and skin, a little out of character, but entirely worth it. The surf cracked clean and even in the distance, where Jared paddled into a rising swell, all smooth power and effortless grace.

She had to laugh at herself: Saturday mornings used to mean bookstores, galleries, and overpriced espressos in misty Seattle cafes. Now she was playing fetch with a dog on a golden Sydney beach, watching her incredibly attractive boss carve waves like something out of a movie. Still, an ache bloomed behind her ribs.

She missed the drizzly walks home, the paper bags full of pastries, and long talks over coffee that somehow lasted three hours. More than anything, she missed Isobel.

Smiling, she checked the time. Lunchtime in Seattle.

Pulling out her phone, she turned her back to the waves and hit Isobel's name. The call connected on the second ring and her best friend's familiar face filled the screen—messy topknot, scarf bundled around her neck, and what looked like a half-finished cocktail in one hand. Music hummed in the background.

"Friday wrap started early, has it?"

Isobel grinned and held up her glass. "Hey, I signed two contracts before noon. I earned this."

Emily laughed. "Are you at Jupiter Bar?"

"Yeah. Lila just dumped a tech bro, so this is technically emotional support." Her eyes narrowed at Emily. "Are you at the beach?"

"Mm-hmm." She angled the camera, catching the crashing waves, and the two surfers hugging their boards as they emerged from the ocean behind her. "Jared's been out surfing with a mate."

Isobel's voice pitched upward. "*That's* not Jared."

"No," Emily said with a smirk, just as Josh appeared at her shoulder, shaking out his wet hair and flashing a grin directly at the camera.

"Hey, Em. Who's your hot friend?"

Emily blinked. "You don't even know who I'm talking to."

Josh shrugged, still grinning. "Does it matter?"

Emily snorted. "Isobel, meet Josh."

Isobel leaned closer to the screen. "Hi, Josh." Then, once he'd disappeared: "Why is it you're always surrounded by hot men, and I'm stuck with hipsters in flannel shackets debating kombucha flavors?"

Emily laughed, her attention scanning for Lucy, but something wasn't right. The dog was no longer at the water's edge. She was halfway up the beach, tail stiff, body low, clearly uncomfortable.

And someone was with her.

Someone in a gray hoodie crouched at her side, gripping her collar like they were trying to control her. She yelped, struggling backward.

"Gotta go." Emily ended the call without hesitation or explanation. "Hey!"

The figure looked up—face shadowed beneath the hood—then bolted.

Jared was already moving. "What the hell—" He sprinted up the beach toward the figure as Lucy tore free and raced back to him, tail between her legs.

Josh didn't wait. He took off, muscles bunching as he disappeared over the dunes.

Emily dropped to her knees beside Jared, running her hands over Lucy's chest and back, checking for injuries. The dog whined softly but didn't pull away. "She's shaken, but I think she's okay."

Then she noticed something.

Tucked just inside Lucy's collar, folded into a neat rectangle, was a slip of paper.

Jared took it from her hand, his expression sharpening as he unfolded it. He read it once, jaw tight, then passed it to her.

Whatever you're digging up—bury it. Or someone might just have to do it for you.

Emily looked up at him, a concerned breath catching in her throat. Jared's arms closed around her without hesitation, pulling her into his chest like it was instinct. "You okay?" he murmured into her hair.

She nodded, but her eyes were still scanning the beach—families setting up for the day, putting up sun tents and laying out towels, a noisy knot of Junior Surf Lifesavers jogging past in bright red caps. Nothing out of the ordinary. But someone had been watching.

Josh returned a moment later, breathless and empty-handed. "Lost him in the parking lot."

"Was it Ethan?" Emily asked quietly.

Josh shook his head. "Didn't get a good look, but I don't think so." He glanced around again, eyes briefly narrowing toward the dunes, then looked back at them. At Jared's arms still wrapped tightly around her. "You know," he added, a slow grin tugging at one side of his mouth, "you're not exactly being subtle."

Emily tensed slightly, but Jared didn't move. He just looked at Josh, steady and unapologetic.

"Relax, boss. Everyone knows," Josh said with a shrug. "And seriously—they don't give a shit. Just be happy, man. Life's too short. Trust me."

He clapped Jared on the shoulder and jogged off with his board, leaving a hum of energy in his wake.

Emily stayed where she was, pressed against Jared's chest, listening to the thud of his heart beneath her cheek. Then his voice dropped low and amused, next to her ear.

"By the way," he said, glancing down, "this bikini should come with a warning."

She tilted her head up, puzzled.

"I didn't realize you were planning to ruin my morning concentration."

"Guess we're even then," she murmured, the corners of her mouth lifting. "You in that wetsuit wasn't exactly helpful either."

He gave a quiet chuckle, and for a moment, the tension bled away.

Back at the loft, the weight of the day hadn't lifted—it had merely shifted. Heavier now, more focused. After mutual reflection, they'd agreed not to involve the police. The note had been a warning, not a threat of action. Just enough to rattle them. And it had worked.

Emily stood by the wide windows, watching the swell of moonlight over the harbor, the shadows longer than they'd been that morning. Jared leaned over the kitchen island, scrolling through a shared document they'd been building all day.

"This isn't just a scandal," she hissed, moving to stack the dishwasher with their plates and discarded coffee mugs. "It's a full-blown cover-up. And the people behind it—they're dangerous."

Jared nodded, his jaw tense. "Which is why we don't blink. We protect the disk. We protect Reed. And we protect each other. That matters more than anything."

That vow hung in the air between them and intensified. The weight of what they'd uncovered had taken on a new shape. Less about the past, and more about the future.

Theirs.

Emily opened the fridge and poured them both a generous

glass of crisp white wine. She took up her place beside him at the counter, looking over their plan for the auction: what to release, how to structure the revelation, and what lines they wouldn't let Pendleton Press cross. By the time the sky outside turned velvet-black, their strategy was almost airtight—but the stakes had never felt higher.

"I'm going to loop Isobel in," Emily said, tapping out a message on her phone. Not only did she feel the need to explain the abrupt ending to their call, but Emily's best friend was a senior brand strategist, known for turning dull campaigns into viral gold. "She'll know how to frame this for the best impact. Her understanding of how imagery and symbolism evoke emotion could elevate the auction into a storytelling powerhouse. If we want the audience to care, we have to make them *feel* it."

Jared paused, looking over at her. "Then we'll need Jess, too."

Emily stilled. "Legal Jess?" Then, before she could stop herself—"Or your ex, Jess?"

He startled—not guilty, exactly, but surprised. Like it hadn't even occurred to him she wouldn't already know.

"Same Jess."

Something sharp tugged at her chest. "You didn't think to tell me this earlier?" She kept her voice steady, but it cost her.

Jared exhaled, closing his laptop. "I get how it looks, Em," he said carefully. "But Jess has been our legal counsel for years—it's not a secret. I guess it just... slipped my mind. Because our past doesn't matter to me. But you're right. I should have told you.

152

And I'm sorry."

Their past might not matter to *him*, but it did to Emily. Not because she didn't trust him, but because learning it like this made her feel foolish. Like she'd missed a piece of the story everyone else already knew.

She looked down at her phone, her pulse too loud in her ears. "Okay."

"Hey." His voice dropped an octave. "Look at me."

She did. And found his gaze burning into hers.

"I'm not the kind of guy who burns bridges." His tone was quiet, deliberate. "Especially not with people who helped shape me. Jess was important to me once, yeah. But she also taught me to fight for what I care about. And she's damn good at what she does. When Pendleton hits back—and they will—we'll need someone who knows how to push harder. That's why I mentioned her. That's the *only* reason."

Emily nodded, but her throat was tight. She wasn't even sure what she needed to hear—just that it wasn't *this*.

Jared watched her for another beat, then spoke softer still. "If things went sideways with us, would you want me to hate you?" A pause. "Because I couldn't."

She didn't answer.

The word *us* was already unraveling her—the tension between them softening into something more dangerous in its intimacy. Hours passed, and they found themselves curled on the couch—Jared's legs stretched over the coffee table, Emily's tucked beneath her. Their thighs pressed close, arms brushing now and then as they passed their laptops back and forth.

The careful lines they'd drawn earlier in the week began to blur completely.

Jared leaned back, raking both hands through his hair. Emily was scrolling through their shared doc—half of it was beautifully organized, color-coded and punctuated; the other half chaotic and half-finished, littered with notes like: [insert item description here].

She smirked, nudging him with her elbow. "You work like your brain's a whiteboard with no eraser."

He gave a small laugh, sheepish. "That's generous. I think it's more like a bomb went off in a library. I usually leave the auction itinerary to Gareth these days. He's the expert and always changes it to suit himself, anyway."

Emily moved a few chunks of text into place, cleaned up a section header, and tilted the screen toward him. "Well. He'll be following this one to the letter. Our success depends on it."

Jared looked at her, a flicker of warmth behind the fatigue. "You're really good at this, you know. I've spent most of my adult life maintaining a facade, trying to convince the world—and maybe even myself—that I have it all figured out. But the truth? I've always been more comfortable living inside the mess."

Emily glanced sideways at him, surprised. "Really?"

He nodded, thoughtful. "Yeah. People think I'm polished because of the job, the name. But the truth is, I grew up in a house ruled by chaos—with a dad who never threw anything out and a mom who could charm a collector out of their heirlooms and make them thank her for it. So I need someone who can create order from the mess." Their eyes locked, the space between them humming with something unspoken—something electric. "I knew you were that person the first moment I met you—lining up in the lobby of that little inn in Leavenworth."

She smiled at the memory. "You pushed in—charmingly, I might add—because you were running late."

"See? But you're not just organized, Em. You're... grounding."

"You mean I'm good at handling your mess."

He grinned. "I mean, I'm hoping you want to."

She tilted her head, the air between them stretching taut. "Is that a compliment or a warning?"

"Maybe both," he said, voice softer now.

Their knees brushed again. Then their shoulders. His thigh against hers. Their proximity shifted, small degrees at a time, until it was impossible not to feel the heat rolling off him.

"This was supposed to be just a job," she said, more to herself than him. Like naming it might bring back some measure of control.

Jared's voice dropped, soft but certain. "Yeah. But we both knew it wasn't—right from the start. The moment you accepted my offer... you were never just passing through."

Another silence bloomed—wider, deeper, more dangerous.

Her heart thudded in her chest, loud against the muted hum

of the night.

With a slow hand, he eased her laptop aside. His gaze dipped to her mouth. Lingered. He was closer than she realized. He leaned in—closer now, close enough that she could feel the words before he spoke them.

"I want you to stay, Em. Not for the job. For me."

She didn't answer with words. She just leaned in, too.

Their lips brushed—barely. Her phone was buzzing, sharp against the silence.

She pulled back, breath catching as she reached for it. Jared caught her wrist gently, his eyes still on her. "Don't," he murmured, like the word alone might hold the moment intact.

But it was too late. She'd already glanced at the screen. "It's Simon," she said, exhaling. "I should—"

He let go.

She answered, putting the phone on speaker. Jared's gaze fixed on her, intense, unreadable.

"Emily," Simon's voice came through, a little raw. "Sorry for the late hour. I finished a draft—something I want to read at the auction. I know what I want to say... I just need someone to tell me if it's right. Will you look at it?"

Her throat tightened. "Of course," she said softly. "Send it through."

As she ended the call, silence settled over the room again, but not like it was before. She turned to Jared. His gaze hadn't left her. Still warm. Still wanting. But whatever had almost happened was gone, slipping like sand between her fingers.

12

Roots in the Ashes

"I had dismissed the old stories, waved them off as superstition. But standing there, in the dark of the forest with the breath of something unseen against my cheek—I was no longer so certain."

~ The Ghosts of Blackwood Ridge

After hours spent replaying Jared's words, sleep had taken its time coming. Because he hadn't said *everything*.

He hadn't said *why* he wanted her to stay.

And as much as it mattered, *"I want you to stay"* wasn't the same as *"I'm falling in love with you."*

Not that she was ready to say it, either. But the truth clung to her, secretive yet undeniable. This was never supposed to be more than a job. And yet here she was, aching for a version of them that didn't have an expiration date.

She padded into the kitchen in her robe, tying it loosely as she went. The scent of fresh coffee greeted her before the sight of Jared leaning on the counter. Dressed down in crisp navy Bermuda shorts and a white linen shirt, his rolled sleeves clung to his biceps in a way that momentarily derailed her thoughts. It was a look she wasn't used to, and it suited him far too well.

He raised his eyes at her approach, raking them over her robe in a way that made her check to see that it wasn't gaping. "Good morning, sleepyhead. I was just about to send Lucy in for a wake-up call."

She took the waiting coffee gratefully. "I almost needed one."

He nodded, then glanced down at Lucy. "Mom and Dad are back from their trip, so I'm taking Luce home today."

"Oh." The word escaped before she could soften it. The disappointment was sharper than expected. "I'll miss her."

Jared's gaze lingered on her face a second longer than it needed to. He stepped closer and laid his hands gently on her waist, the heat of them seeping through the silk of her gown. "Come with me."

Emily straightened, her brows lifting. "You want me to meet your parents?"

He shrugged, casual—but not entirely. "Why not? Only if you're up for it, though. No pressure."

She tilted her head, skeptical. "What if they don't like me?"

He smirked. "They'll love you. Dad will probably corner you about obscure French estates or detail every single step of their trip. And Mom... well, just be yourself. She can spot a fake from all the way across the harbor."

Emily gave a slow, mock-serious nod. "Good thing I'm excellent under pressure."

"Good thing," he echoed, brushing a strand of hair from her face. "Because we're leaving in fifteen minutes."

The Bell family home sat tucked behind a tall hedge on a leafy street in Woollahra, the kind of place that hinted at wealth without announcing it. Sandstone walls, wraparound veranda, and—Emily noted as they walked up the steps—a polished brass bell, complete with a porcelain pull handle painted in a delicate blue-and-white Spode pattern. Jared gave it a gentle tug, prompting a volley of frantic barks from Lucy.

Margot Bell answered the door a moment later, her ash-blonde hair swept back in a loose twist, linen pants cinched at the waist, and a sleeveless silk blouse in pale coral. She took one look at her son, who was still laughing at Lucy's outburst, and scowled good-naturedly. "Very funny."

She continued to study Emily with a discerning eye as they stepped inside. "You must be the new curator from the States."

Emily offered a small, genuine smile as she extended her hand. "Emily Sloane. It's lovely to meet you, Mrs. Bell. You have a beautiful home."

Margot took her hand with a polite nod, but it was the slight lift of her brow that gave Emily pause—subtle, controlled.

Instantly recognizable. Jared had the same tell when sizing someone up.

"Thank you, Emily," she said. Then, with a teasing lilt: "Though I might suggest leaving work at the door next time. You've been mentally cataloging everything since you crossed the threshold."

Emily froze for half a second, then laughed, a little embarrassed. "Guilty. I guess I don't have an off switch."

Margot's smirk softened into something gentler. "Don't worry. Takes one to know one." She gave Emily a small, knowing shrug as she moved into the living room. "I was a curator in another life—until I realized the real fun is in the chase."

Jared gave a snort. "And before she started acquiring entire wineries while on vacation."

Margot didn't miss a beat. "Some stories are worth preserving in more than one format."

Jared's father, James, joined them, barefoot in rolled chinos and a designer polo shirt. His hair was silvering, but his smile was instant and easy.

"Emily, how lovely to finally meet you," he said, offering a warm shake of her hand. "We heard there was a brilliant woman behind Jared's new direction. Didn't expect she'd also be this lovely."

Jared groaned. "Dad, please."

James grinned, then bent to scratch behind Lucy's ears. The dog wagged her tail furiously, thudding against the polished floorboards. "Well, Lucy seems to like you," James said, glancing up at Emily. "And if that's not an excellent judge of character, I don't know what is."

"Lucy also likes snacks," Margot chimed in from the hall, her voice dry.

"Yeah, well—Emily is the whole snack platter," Jared murmured with a wink, his hand resting on her lower back as he gestured for her to follow them further inside.

She wasn't sure what she'd expected from Jared's childhood home. He'd once described it as "a museum of inherited clutter," so she'd braced for rooms stacked with antiques and faded grandeur. But the house was high-ceilinged and sun-drenched, filled with pieces that bore the patina of long stories. The front room held antique armchairs reupholstered in modern linen, a grandfather clock that ticked in polite rhythm, and art-lined walls where oil portraits mingled with minimalist prints. The air smelled faintly of lemon polish and eucalyptus.

Despite the family's legacy, the home didn't feel like a museum—it felt lived in. Every object had its place, but the overall feel was relaxed, collected. Warm.

In the kitchen, Jared poured iced sparkling water while James leaned on the marble island. "How were the waves this morning?" he asked his son, picking up a twist of lemon and dropping it in his glass.

"Didn't go," Jared replied. "Josh and I dropped the boards in yesterday, though. Today's all about auction prep."

"How's it coming along?"

Jared glanced at Emily, caught her eye, and she gave him a quick nod. "We should probably give you a heads-up about Tuesday night," he said.

James raised a brow, half curious. "Something more dramatic than champagne and record-breaking bids?"

"Yes, actually," Emily said, her tone light. "We've made a few changes to the format. It's going to be much more than just an auction."

Margot's lips curved in mild interest. "More than an auction?" She took a slow sip of her drink, before setting the glass down. "Bell's has seen its fair share of changes over the years—I'd like to think we're adaptable. But upheaval—well, that tends to linger in ways people don't always expect."

Emily exchanged another glance with Jared. His expression was encouraging, even admirable. "The Barrow collection has a unique legacy. We owe it to him to present it accordingly."

Margot ran a curious and not-too-subtle eye over Emily. "I suppose it depends on the kind of change you're bringing."

There was definitely something assessing in her tone, not wary exactly, more reflective—like she was measuring the weight of Emily's presence, the energy of someone young enough to shake things up, old enough to know exactly how.

Margot's attention shifted to James, briefly, something unreadable passing between them before she looked back at Emily, her smile deepening. "What exactly makes this auction... more?"

"The headline item has a rather complicated provenance,"

Jared explained. "One that won't just shake the literary crowd—it could ruffle some much bigger feathers."

James set down his glass, attention sharpening. "How ruffled are we talking?"

"We have evidence of coercion by Victor Barrow's publisher that directly impacted his health." He let the weight of that settle before continuing. "The auction won't just be a sale—it'll be a stage. The first time the truth is laid out for the public, where it can't be buried or spun."

James frowned slightly, absorbing the implications. "And you're sure this is the best route?"

Emily spoke gently. "This just isn't about Barrow. It affects other employees and their families, giving them the space to finally speak the truth without legal implications. I'm sure you'd agree that if the public is bidding on Barrow's legacy items, they should know exactly what they're paying for."

Margot's gaze flicked between them. "I won't even ask how you got your hands on all that information." She turned to Jared, her expression sharp. "Jess agreed to this?"

Jared gave a small, grounding nod. "We're taking every precaution. There's already NDAs in place and Josh is across the security. We have tight access, vetted invites, and Jess has partners on standby, ensuring this doesn't implode before it even begins. We just didn't want you walking in blind."

James's expression didn't shift much—but the glint in his eye turned thoughtful. "We stand by what's right, Jared. You know that."

"I do. That's why we're doing this." He leaned closer to Emily and reached for her hand. She squeezed back.

James nodded slowly. "Alright then, son. We'll be there behind you."

"There's just one more thing." Jared grinned, causing Margot to raise her brow. "Could you bring Lucy? We need her to help tell the story, and I don't want her shedding all over my tux."

Margot blinked at her son. "The dog is part of the event?" Her mouth tugged sideways—not quite a frown, more like restrained curiosity. "That's... unexpected."

"We need it to be."

Margot gave a short, approving hum. "Just don't expect her to wear one of those ridiculous bows again."

"No bows," Jared promised, grinning.

Emily watched all this quietly—how swiftly the conversation shifted into alignment, without drama, or posturing. Just steady ground beneath a risky step. And maybe, she thought, that was what made this family powerful. Not just wealth or legacy, but trust.

The kind of foundation you could stand on.

They settled around a huge white-oak dining table on the Bells' patio, Emily reflecting on how eating alfresco seemed to be an Aussie tradition. Lunch was simple—grilled fish, crisp summer salad, and a chilled bottle of Verdelho that James poured with a practiced hand.

"So, Portugal again, huh?" Jared picked up his glass with a wry smile, twirling its contents and sniffing its bouquet like a true connoisseur. "This another one of your souvenirs?"

Margot shot her son a warning glance as she reached for the vinaigrette. "Not this time."

"Now that sounds suspiciously like a story," Emily mused with a grin.

James chuckled, wiping his hands on his napkin. "Well, the last time we were there..." He paused for effect, his gaze flicking between them as if gauging how much trouble he wanted to stir up.

Margot sighed, but there was amusement behind it. "Oh, here we go."

James grinned, eyes alight with the kind of playful nostalgia that proved Jared right on his dad's love for storytelling. "Let's just say that while visiting a contact in Porto, we took a detour to the Douro Valley for what was meant to be one wine tasting."

"Which turned into four," Margot added without looking up from her plate.

"Five," James corrected. "And before I knew it, we'd somehow agreed to buy a pair of dusty old wine crates that the vineyard had tucked away in a storage barn. Margot spotted them during the tour."

"They were 19th century with original stenciling! They weren't for sale, of course, but I made them an offer they couldn't refuse."

Emily laughed. "That's one way to antique. Do you still have them?"

Margot gestured through to the living room. Tucked neatly beneath a wide console table were the crates—cleaned up and now repurposed as cushion and blanket storage. "They were too good to be used as donkey feeders," she said with a small shrug.

"That's them?" Emily exclaimed. Before she could stop herself, she had gone inside for a closer look. "May I?" she asked Margot, who nodded.

Tentatively, she brushed her receptive hand across the wood—feeling the softness of the aged timber, and the now-faded paint. Through her touch, Emily's mind filled with a scene, vivid as though she were truly there.

> *A young apprentice bends over the pinewood crate, the air thick with the scent of sawdust and oil paint. In one hand, he holds a worn stencil carved from thin sheet metal, its edges slightly battered from use. He dips a small, bristled brush into a pot of black paint, before moving it in short, deliberate dabs, filling the negative spaces of the lettering. When he lifts the stencil, the words "Casa das Encostas" gleams freshly on the wood, a name imbued with dignity and the weight of tradition.*

The vision only lasted a second or so, and as Emily's fingers traced the lettering, Margot spoke up as though reading her thoughts. "It means 'House of the Hillsides,'" she said, her voice ringing with pride. "A name as rooted in the land as the vines themselves."

After witnessing their craftmanship, Emily looked at the crates with new appreciation.

"They're really lovely," she said as they returned to the table.

"They're useful," Margot corrected, and with a pointed look at James, added, "Lovely is merely a bonus."

Jared lowered his voice, leaning close so only Emily could hear. "Told you she doesn't miss much."

She turned to find him watching her, a contented smile on his face. She wasn't sure if it was pride, affection, or something deeper—but it made her heart lift.

Jared stretched slightly, shifting his weight like he was ready to move.

James gave him a firm clap on the shoulder. "We'll see you Tuesday, then."

Emily stood, instinctively reaching for the nearest plate.

Margot caught the movement immediately. "Oh, sweetheart, don't worry about that." She shook her head, already stacking the dishes herself. "You're a guest—just relax."

Emily hesitated, fingers brushing the edge of her glass before she pulled back, swallowing the sudden weight in her chest. She was sure Margot didn't mean to offend. More like Margot hadn't even considered that Emily might belong in the rhythm of clearing up, a rhythm that Jared moved through easily, gathering the plates without hesitation.

But the reminder lingered. She hadn't earned her place in the Bell family. Not yet.

"Thank you for lunch," Emily said, her voice warm but quieter than before. "I really enjoyed meeting you both."

"You're welcome, Emily. We're sorry we weren't here to welcome you on arrival, but it was all rather sudden." Margot offered her a small smile, not quite warm, but sincere. "But it's nice to see someone keeping Jared on his toes."

As they bid their farewells and stepped out into the warm afternoon sunshine, Emily exhaled. "I like them."

Jared shot her a sideways glance. "Even Mom?"

"Especially your mom," she said, then hesitated. "Do you think I passed?"

"Oh, you definitely passed," he said, unlocking the Porsche with a barely audible click. "And if Lucy's still choosing to sit beside you instead of Dad, you may have stolen the family loyalty outright."

Emily smiled, but the earlier uncertainty still lingered, pressing at the edges of her confidence. She couldn't afford to screw up—not with so much riding on this auction. Jared may have been the director, but James and Margot's influence ran deep, woven into the very foundation of the family business.

Yet, it was more than just about proving herself. In this vast, untamed land, where she had no family and only the tentative bonds of friendship with Jared—and perhaps Sofia—she felt the ache of something more. She was hungry for connection, and if she were being completely honest with herself—she wanted to be worthy of Jared, too.

They were halfway home, the afternoon sun slanting gold across the dash, when Jared's phone lit up on the console.

Jess.

Emily's stomach tightened. The name alone pulled her straight back to the conversation they hadn't quite finished—about honesty, about transparency. About the fact that he hadn't told her he and Jess were still working together. Not until she'd asked.

Jared's hand found hers, his fingers warm and steady as he touched his earpiece to answer the call. "Hey, Jess. What's going on?" The glance he gave her was soft, apologetic. "You've finished looking over Simon's speech?" he clarified aloud, for her benefit.

Emily sat up straighter. "And?"

There was a pause while he listened—nodding slightly, brows drawing together in thought. Then he ended the call, saying, "She says it's strong. Brave, actually. But she has a counter-suggestion. A proposal for you."

Emily blinked. "For me?" Including Jared's initial request to work for him—"That makes two proposals in a month," she said, flashing him a small smile.

"What can I say?" he said with a grin. "I'm not the only one who wants you."

His admission barely had time to settle—just long enough for the meaning to linger—before his tone shifted. More serious now.

"Jess thinks it's best if Simon doesn't deliver the speech himself. It could be too risky. He needs a Bell's representative to speak for him."

Emily nodded, heart already catching up. "Of course. I'll find someone."

Jared hesitated, then turned to her fully as they paused at a traffic light. "She thinks it should be you."

"What?" She stared at him. "Me? On stage?"

"You know the material inside out. Better than that, you can deliver the emotion better than anyone, having experienced it directly."

He was right, of course. When was he not? Her visions had given her a unique perspective no one else, not even Simon Reed, could portray. Something Margot said to her son earlier now resonated. *Some stories are worth preserving in more than one format.*

"I thought I was producing the show, not headlining it." Her laugh was thin. "Besides, I didn't pack anything that complements a tux."

"You're perfect for this," Jared said, his voice soft but sure. "And don't worry—I already took care of the dress."

She shot him a disbelieving look.

He smirked, squeezing her thigh gently. "Trust me."

That evening, Emily and Jared worked from opposite ends of the couch, laptops open, bare feet tangled somewhere in the middle. The low notes of instrumental music played in the background—piano, but unobtrusive.

Final descriptions were tweaked. Timelines triple-checked. Staging set with precision. Emily found herself watching Jared sometimes when he wasn't looking—the crease between his brows, the small flex of his jaw when he concentrated. She saw his parents in him now, unmistakably. The perfectionism. The need for control. But she also saw where he diverged. He wasn't brittle. He was curious. And under all that polish, hungry for meaning.

She opened a chat bubble with Isobel on her screen.

> Sending you final requests for staging + visuals. Just the last three slides. You're a genius. Don't fight me on it.

She watched the typing ellipsis bounce once... disappear... bounce again. She frowned, not expecting Isobel to answer immediately. It was nearing 2:30 a.m. on Sunday back home. *Seattle isn't home anymore*, she reminded herself. Here—Sydney—this was home.

For now.

> You're lucky I like you.

> It's before dawn on a SUNDAY—are you caffeinated or possessed?

> A bit of both.

Emily grinned. She'd known Isobel Kendrick since freshman year at UW and she'd always been the bold one, the hype woman, the ride-or-die who tells it straight. A quick glance at Jared showed him preoccupied for the minute. Before she could change her mind, her fingers flew across the keyboard.

> Also… J bought me a dress. For Tuesday night. Without asking.

> He bought you a dress??? I don't know if that's chivalrous or chauvinist.

> I KNOW, RIGHT??? I'm spinning on it. He's already bought it—like it was obvious.

> Okay, but… is it obviously good? Like, did he nail your taste?

I haven't even seen it yet.

But wait—it gets messier.

Oh no.

He's still in touch with his ex. She's this really stunning older Brit. Extremely put together. Did I mention stunning.

You did.

Please tell me this isn't a deep dive into her LinkedIn.

Nope. Worse. She does his legals.

AND he used to read her Trixie Belden books.

In BED, Issy.

What? HOW do you know that?

It came out in conversation. But... I also kind of confirmed the bed thing in a vision.

EMILY.

I know. I KNOW.

I didn't mean to pry—it just surfaced. Like it wanted to be seen.

You didn't MEAN to? Em, that's not how vision work is supposed to go.

Consent, remember?

I feel like an imposter.

He's so composed, and I'm just an open wound with art degrees.

First of all: rude to yourself.

Second: you're brilliant and gorgeous and he knows it.

Third: Reading in bed? Boring.

Surely you're not that unsatisfied?

We've only kissed a handful of times.

Wow. Okay.

Maybe he's just old-school?

He has a professional facade to maintain. He's probably just being respectful.

You think?

I'd rather be his dirty little secret.

Dirty can be fun!

But you met his parents today, didn't you? That's a thing. A CAPITAL-T Thing.

How did that go, btw?

It was good!

His mom's a little reserved, but I think I made it through without embarrassing myself too much.

Although she totally caught me checking out all her stuff. So awkward.

Ha. Classic. Moms see everything.

Anyway—real question. How'd it end with the ex?

She ended it. Apparently outgrew him.

Ouch. That'll do it.

He's probably just guarding his heart now.

I just don't want to mess it up.

I feel like I'm already halfway there.

You're not. You care. That's not a flaw.

Look, this goes against everything I stand for-

But take it slow.

Enjoy the burn.

The typing ellipsis disappeared, leaving Emily to savor those last three lingering words.

She exhaled slowly, her thoughts tangled between Isobel's message and Jared's silent presence across from her. His eyes found hers, holding her gaze for a fraction too long, before offering a small questioning smile.

Emily's heart fluttered—not from the words or the silence, but from the realization that Issy was right. Some fires don't demand fanning; they burn hotter when left unattended.

13

Behind the Curtain

"And there, just beyond the lantern's reach,
I saw it—a hulking shadow with eyes like
smoldering embers, its breath curling in the
night air like a whispered curse. I knew then
that to run was folly, for the Blackwood
Horror does not chase. It waits."
Simon Reed ~ Return to Blackwood Vale

"... And so, The Hound of Blackwood Vale is no mere phantom—it is a manifestation of avarice, born from Blackwood's darkest history and bound to those who dare to exploit its legacy. Legends whisper that the beast is the revenant of a forgotten guardian, once a flesh-and-blood creature twisted into something unnatural by centuries of greed, betrayal, and blood spilled over Blackwood's cursed land.

It is said that long ago, the Blackwood estate was built atop sacred ground, never meant to be disturbed—a place where something ancient slumbered. When men sought to claim it for themselves, carving their names into its history, they awoke the Hound.

But its hunger is not for flesh alone. The Hound does not simply kill—it haunts, it torments, it drives its victims to ruin, much as Pendleton Press has done to those who dared to wield their own voices against it. Just as Victor Barrow was stripped of his agency, and Simon Reed manipulated into obscurity, the Hound serves as a dark mirror of the cycle: the more the truth is buried, the stronger it becomes.

It does not come for the innocent. It comes for those who covet, who take without thought of consequence. And now, as Victor Barrow's intrepid detective, Elias Thorne, prepares to return to Blackwood Vale, the Hound stirs once more—not merely as a specter of the past, but as an omen of what is yet to come."

Emily sat for a long time on the edge of the makeshift stage, Reed's speech resting in her lap, its weight pressing into her like a stone. She had read through it three times now. Not just for clarity or tone, but to feel it. To absorb the quiet devastation in his words, the long-held truths stitched carefully between each paragraph.

This wasn't just his story.

It was a reckoning. Not a confession, but a raw, unflinching truth—laid bare without shame. A call for justice. For Victor. For what had been taken from them both.

"It's powerful," she'd told him Saturday night when he'd first sent it through. "It feels like closure, but also... like a beginning."

He had thanked her, grateful that she'd understood what he was trying to do.

"Are you sure you're ready for this?" she'd asked.

His answer, when it finally came, only strengthened her resolve: "I think I have been for a long time."

Emily swallowed the lump in her throat and closed the folder. She had flown halfway around the world for a job, and instead, had found something far more dangerous: conviction.

In Reed's words. In her own future.

Because the truth—once unearthed—could change everything. And that knowledge crackled like static in her veins.

All around her, preparations for tomorrow night's auction were underway. Lights were being rigged, chairs precisely spaced, and entire sets constructed across the polished timber stage where she sat. The venue—a cavernous, repurposed heritage gallery tucked in the street behind the auction house—had been Emily's choice, on Jared's advice. Bell's had a standing arrangement with the gallery, and for good reason. Their own auction rooms, elegant though they were, would never have handled the scale of this production.

Here, though, Isobel's vision had room to breathe. The space was being transformed into a gothic, forested wilderness—Blackwood Vale brought to life. Her concept of leading guests through a series of immersive "vignettes," each echoing Barrow's world and anchoring key auction items, was daring. The kind of creative risk that would make industry purists like Pendleton twitch. Which, frankly, was part of the appeal. Barrow's fans, however, would eat it up.

Emily walked the gallery floor slowly. Let her heels echo. Let the weight of tomorrow evening settle into her bones.

She ran through the presentation deck Isobel had sent—clicking through images from the auction catalog and a few snapshots she'd taken while at the Channings', such as the view from Victor's writing room, and the empty pedestal, left forlorn and foreboding. Here, the haunting music halted abruptly.

When the final slide faded to a quote from Reed's forthcoming biography of Barrow—and Lucy's cue to materialize on stage—Emily's chest seized.

That night, back in the loft, Jared cooked—a rich mushroom risotto with cracked pepper and shaved parmesan—the kind of meal that made up for things left unspoken.

Vivaldi spilled throughout the loft, bright and looping. She'd told him once—back in Washington—that it helped her think. He'd remembered.

And maybe that was enough to let the dress slide.

She leaned against the counter as he stirred the risotto, watching the steady movement of his hands. "So, did you at least think about asking me first?"

He didn't look up, just smirked slightly. "Briefly."

Emily huffed, more amused than annoyed. "Right. And you decided my taste isn't suitable?"

"No," Jared said simply, turning off the heat. "I wanted you to walk into that auction feeling exactly like someone who knows she belongs."

His insight landed in a way she hadn't expected—low, certain. She swallowed, shifting in place. "And you're sure I'm going to love it?"

Now, he glanced up, something hot and knowing in his expression. "I'd bet on it."

They shifted to the tiny balcony, and dined under the stars, the city glittering beyond. She kicked off her heels under the table. His shirt was half undone, his sleeves already rolled, warm fingers brushing hers as he passed the wine.

They clinked glasses, and he said, "To truth," without looking away from her.

She paused. "And to whatever's left after it."

"This isn't what you pictured, is it?" he asked her.

Emily blinked. "What do you mean?"

"Coming out here. Only to get caught up in all of this scandal." His voice lowered to something softer as he twirled the stem of his glass. "Did you ever think you'd end up in the middle of a mess like mine?"

She let out a soft laugh, shaking her head. "Not exactly."

Jared smirked, taking a slow sip of his wine. "So, what did you picture yourself doing?"

"Apart from flying across the country in your private jet?" she teased. Her introduction to the world of Bell's Fine Auctions had been a little unorthodox, to say the least. "I had no idea, to be honest. I just knew that you'd allow me to trust my instincts more than I ever could as a museum curator. To be more than just some assistant fussing over antiques and artifacts, but someone who got to shape what people saw. What stories got told."

Jared hummed. "So, basically, *this*—but without the chaos?"

"Pretty much." She laughed, softer this time.

He smirked. "And here you are, helping shape a whole different kind of story."

Emily traced the stem of her glass, gaze flickering between him and the city beyond. "What about you? Was the directorship of the family company always on the horizon?"

Jared didn't answer right away. He exhaled slowly, watching the way the wine swirled in his glass, the movement lazy, deliberate. "Not always," he said finally. "Acquisitions was where I thought I'd end up. You nailed it earlier. I've always had an eye for beautiful things."

His gaze locked onto hers, something teasing, something slow. "Of course, I also aspired to be a chef. But thankfully, that wasn't my future. It could have been disastrous."

Emily tossed down her napkin and met his eyes head-on. "Are you kidding? You're a great cook. This risotto is *perfection*."

To prove her point, she scooped up another forkful, savoring the bite before she swallowed. Jared grinned, tucking into his own plate, but she caught him watching her as she ate—more than once—until curiosity got the better of her.

She lifted a brow. "What?"

Jared just kept looking at her, expression unreadable but edged with amusement.

"Do I have food on my face or something?"

Jared shook his head, still holding that same quiet intensity. "No," he said finally, setting his glass down. "I just like watching you enjoy things."

Emily blinked, caught somewhere between surprise and something warmer, deeper.

"So," she said, tilting her head, "does that mean you get some kind of satisfaction knowing I'm savoring *your* risotto?"

His lips curved, slow, deliberate. "What do your instincts tell you?"

She rolled her eyes but couldn't quite suppress the smile, leaning back in her chair. "I think you just like the ego boost."

Jared smirked, reaching for the wine bottle, refilling her glass before his own. "Maybe. Or maybe I just like knowing I got *something* right today."

Emily traced the rim of her glass, studying him. "You did," she said softly. "You got more than just this right."

He cleared his throat, leaned forward. "I bet you're nervous."

Emily let out a breath of a laugh. "You're not?"

"I'm terrified," he admitted. "But not about the speech. Not even the fallout."

Her eyes met his. "Then what?"

"That it'll change the way you feel about us. That this—whatever this is—won't be enough after. You've had one hell of a baptism of fire. You sure it's not too much?"

Her heart clenched. She reached for his hand, threading their fingers together.

"Jared Bell," she said softly. "If you think I'm walking away from this—*from you*—you haven't been paying attention."

He looked at her like he was seeing her not as the woman he'd pulled into the chaos, but as the one who was leading him out of it.

For a long moment, neither of them moved. The distance between them felt taut, humming with everything unspoken. The very air itself charged.

It would've taken nothing—less than nothing—for him to pull her into his lap, to bury his hands in her hair. For her to unbutton the rest of his shirt and abandon the logic that said *not yet*.

On any other night, it could've happened.

On any other night, it *would've*.

But not tonight.

Tonight wasn't about giving in to heat or hunger. It was about choosing patience over impulse—honoring the weight of everything that had brought them here. Trust was still settling into the cracks between them, fragile and new.

So, when Jared pressed a kiss to her forehead, slow and reverent, and turned to clear the dishes, something inside her settled.

Not in surrender, but in certainty.

They weren't rushing toward a spark just to watch it burn out. They were building something slower. Hotter. A bonfire that required careful tending.

And even though she wanted to throw herself onto it, she wouldn't. Not until every ember meant something.

Because when that time came, it wouldn't just burn.

It would blaze.

14

Where It All Began

*"The bravest thing a person can do is write
their own name into the story they were told
to admire from afar."*

Emily Sloane

Early light spilled across the loft's polished concrete floors in soft golden streaks.

The city hadn't yet found its full rhythm, but her pulse had.

She rolled out of bed, still in her underwear, and padded toward the wardrobe—and then stopped.

Hanging on the door was a black garment bag, her name written on the card in Jared's familiar scrawl. She plucked it free.

YOU'RE THE BRAVEST PERSON I KNOW.
OWN IT TONIGHT.
— J x

Carefully, she unzipped the bag.

The dress inside made her breath catch. Deep emerald green, cut from liquid silk that caught the light like the surface of a lake at dusk. It was sleeveless with a plunging V-neck, the bodice pleated in a way that sculpted her waist and flared into a floor-length skirt that moved like water.

Emily let her fingers skim the fabric, reverent. Jared hadn't just nailed her taste—every pleat, every line, every inch of the dress told her he'd been paying attention. To who she was, and who she was becoming.

This wasn't just a gift. It was a quiet kind of revelation. A reminder that someone was in her corner—and had been all along.

And with that knowing came a steadiness. Not for the auction, not yet.

But for the day ahead—for the work that had brought her here in the first place.

So for now, she dressed plainly, gathered her hair into a knot, and headed down to the one place that had started all of this: the storage room on sub-level three.

It looked almost exactly as it had a week ago. Like time had hit pause.

The same long aisles. The same stuffed shelves. The same overhead hum.

Emily moved between the rows until she reached the cleared space where she had stood on her very first day. Where, among the rest of Victor Barrow's collection, she'd come face to face with a hellhound.

She stretched a palm out into the empty space. This was where it had begun—not just the discovery, but the belief. The moment she'd stopped waiting to be given a voice and decided to use her own.

Footsteps echoed behind her, only this time she didn't turn.

"I thought I'd find you here," Jared said.

He appeared beside her, a coffee in one hand. His collar was loose around his neck, the sleeves of his dress shirt rolled up. He looked like he hadn't slept, and yet carried the kind of energy only adrenaline—and maybe pride—could summon.

Emily looked up, smiling softly. "Didn't realize I was becoming predictable."

"I don't think you ever could," he said, offering her the coffee. She took it and sipped. Warm, sweet, a little too strong—just like him.

For a moment, they stood in silence, shoulder to shoulder, surrounded by wood and steel and the ghosts of stories not yet told.

"I don't say it enough," Jared said finally, voice low. "But thank you—for being the one who saw this through. I know I've asked a lot of you when I promised not to work you too hard."

She glanced at him. "We asked a lot of each other."

"I just wanted to see you before the madness started." His voice dropped a little. "Remind you what you're walking into that room with."

He reached out and brushed a strand of hair from her face, his fingers lingering at her jaw. Then, without rush or hesitation, he kissed her—slow and sure. A quiet claim. Not possession, but recognition.

When they parted, his thumb traced her cheekbone briefly. "I'll see you tonight."

She didn't watch him go. Just closed her eyes, held the coffee to her lips, and stood in the silence a little longer. She didn't need to rehearse the speech. There was no slideshow to finesse, no last-minute disaster to contain. The work was done. The stage was set. The only thing left was to show up.

And when she did, she wouldn't be the woman who had stood here before, nerves fraying at the edges, questioning her own authority with every step.

Because back then, she'd been trying to prove she belonged.

Now, she *knew* she did.

Golden hour hit the city like a blessing.

Emily arrived at the venue just as the sun dipped behind the skyline, setting fire to the glass facade. Her hair was swept up. Her heels were low and elegant. And the green dress flowed around her like a promise.

A message pinged on her phone as she ascended the stairs.

The stage is yours, curator. Burn it down.

Emily found Jared speaking with Josh near one of the arched entrances on the gallery floor. If she thought he looked devilishly handsome in only a pair of sleep shorts, it had nothing on him in his tux. His hands were pocketed, showing off the breadth of his shoulders, his jaw clean-shaven, tie slightly askew. He looked more like a jewel-thief than someone about to make history.

He turned when he saw her, and whatever he'd been about to say must've caught in his throat. He stared for a moment too long. "You're breathtaking," he said eventually.

She moved closer and reached for his tie, straightening it gently. "There," she murmured, her hand brushing the satin lapel of his jacket. "Lupin himself would be envious."

He caught her hand in his own, holding it against his chest. "Ready to set the room on fire?" he whispered.

Emily looked past him, toward the stage that would change everything. Then back at the man who'd made the space for her to be brave.

She nodded, smoothing her hands down the dress.

"Let's light the match."

15

The Hounding of Victor Barrow

"In the end, it wasn't the whispers of Victor Barrow's own mind that tormented him, nor the beast that prowled within his pages—it was the constant psychological manipulation, the subtle erosion of his trust, and the slow, suffocating pressure to expose the lies that were buried too deep. And just like the beast, that burden was relentless—always at his heels, always hounding the truth."

Simon Reed ~ The Hounding of Victor Barrow:

A Biography

The stage lights went down as Emily uttered the last words of Simon's speech. Each syllable threaded through the room like something living.

Silence followed—not the empty kind, but the charged kind, the kind that grips a space in its jaws and refuses to let go. The kind that means something has shifted. People adjusted in their seats—not in discomfort, but in recognition. In quiet realization that the ground beneath them had moved. And now, nothing sat where it had before.

Simon Reed's words had unraveled everything they thought they knew—about Victor Barrow, about authorship, about truth. No longer a shadowy ghostwriter, Reed had stepped into the light—not to claim fame, but to return it to those denied.

The Hound of Blackwood Vale wasn't just a mere character. It was a vessel. A shared identity. And tonight, it had a face.

Somewhere in the second row, a Pendleton executive gripped the arms of his chair like it might levitate. Across the room, collectors, fans, and curious bidders wore expressions ranging from disbelief to feverish excitement. Whispers moved among them like smoke: *"Did you know?"* *"They really kept this buried for decades?"*

And from her place on center stage, Emily watched the moment unfold—part architect, part witness. She didn't know how it would all end. Only that it was bigger than legacy. This was *justice*.

A spotlight illuminated the lectern, and all eyes turned to Gareth Macallister, Bell's senior auctioneer, whose gavel rested on top like a conductor's baton waiting to orchestrate the crescendo. With a quick adjustment of his tie and a composed smile, he called the room to order.

Lot 1: The Writer's Desk and Chair

Victor Barrow's original writing desk and chair, salvaged from his study after his passing. Oak, deeply worn. Stains from ink. Creak in the left leg of the chair.

"Opening at two thousand," Gareth said, his loud Scottish burr echoing off the bare walls. "Do I hear twenty-five?"

Bidding started strong and stayed there. A paddle lifted. Then another.

"Three thousand. Thirty-five. Four—four-five. Five thousand from the left."

A fierce volley of paddles shot up across the room, the final hammer drop echoing like a note of triumph at seven thousand dollars. The winning bid coming from a private museum in Melbourne.

Lot 2: Original Manuscript Drafts

Multiple annotated drafts of the *Blackwood* series, replete with early revisions and notes between Victor Barrow and his late editor, Franklin Graves.

The room fell into a hush as the lot was unveiled. On

the screen, page after page flickered into view—these were the messy, glorious blueprints of the work that had shaped a generation. The dog-eared corners and whole passages scratched through in haste. Margins crowded with suggestions, revisions layered over earlier thoughts like sediment. And threaded through it all, the secret, desperate correspondence between a doomed author and the editor who had tried—word by word, line by line—to protect him from the shadows closing in.

"Opening at twenty-five hundred," Gareth boomed. "Three thousand. Thirty-five. Four."

Pendleton entered the ring, bidding fast and hard. An agent near the back lifted a hand in response, phone pressed tightly to their ear. The bids climbed steadily, each increment drawing a ripple of intrigue through the room. Pendleton and the agent traded volleys up to eight thousand seven hundred and fifty—then, suddenly, Pendleton stopped.

No hesitation. No sign of calculation. Just... done.

The agent gave a final nod at nine thousand, and the bid held—the crowd responding with polite applause.

Emily's brows knit as her gaze swept the floor, trying to make sense of Pendleton's abrupt retreat. Something wasn't adding up.

From the side of the room, Jess moved with sudden urgency, phone to her ear, her mouth set in a hard line. She didn't speak—but whatever she was hearing had clearly changed the game.

Lot 3: First Editions (Signed and Sealed)

A complete set of Victor Barrow first editions, including *The Hound of Blackwood Vale*—a signed copy long presumed lost, now verified as one of only six in existence.

The books, housed in archival casings, were flawless: uncracked spines, ink as sharp as the day it dried. A testament to care—and obsession. For collectors of rare horror literature, this was holy ground.

"Opening at eight," the Gareth announced.

Bidding started fast. Ten. Twelve. Twelve-five. A sharp nod from the back pushed it to thirteen. A woman in the front, maybe early thirties, didn't hesitate—fifteen.

There was a hum in the room now. Recognition. This wasn't just a lot—it was a legacy.

"Sixteen," called the back.

The woman raised her paddle again. "Seventeen."

Silence. Then, a murmur as the auctioneer called once... twice...

"Sold. Seventeen thousand dollars."

A ripple of applause followed. The woman sat still, blinking fast. Her lips parted, but no sound came. It wasn't joy, exactly—something more sacred. She kept her eyes on the display case along the perimeter wall, where her newly-won books still sat under glass, as though afraid they'd vanish before she could hold them.

Emily, watching from the stage, felt the weight of the moment settle in her chest. This wasn't just a sale. It was a promise—that Victor's work, and the truth behind it, wouldn't be forgotten. Tonight wasn't only about revelations. It was about giving his legacy back to the people who would carry it forward.

Lot 4: Remington Model 5 Typewriter (c. 1939)

An impeccably preserved vintage Remington, allegedly used by Victor Barrow to type all original manuscripts for submission. This iconic piece of literary history bears subtle wear on the keys and platen, a testament to its storied past. Accompanied by a certificate of provenance, the typewriter is not only a relic of craftsmanship but a part of the *Blackwood* legacy.

Gareth adjusted his glasses and smiled at the murmuring crowd. "We'll begin the bidding at three thousand dollars."

"Thirty-five." A paddle shot up near the back.

"Forty-two," a crisp firm voice called from the left.

Gareth raised his voice slightly, reading the room. "Do I hear forty-six?"

A pause—and then, from near the center aisle, a paddle lifted, the bidder's crisp black blazer revealing a forearm inked with intricate script. The bidder sat angled just slightly, face obscured by the row in front.

"Forty-six hundred. Thank you, sir. Do I hear five?"

A slight pause. A nod from the left.

"Then let's move—fifty-two hundred? Yes, thank you."

Josh, standing near the far exit, squinted as the paddle lowered. His hand twitched toward his radio but stopped. Still, his gaze didn't leave the bidder.

"Fifty-eight hundred. Do I hear six?" Gareth's voice pressed upward, the room leaning with it.

Another lift of the inked arm. "Six thousand two hundred," Gareth confirmed with a nod, eyes sharp beneath the stage lights. "Any advance on sixty-two?"

Another pause. No response.

With a last glance around the hall, Gareth's gavel came down. "Sold. To the gentleman near the aisle for six thousand, two hundred dollars."

The bidder didn't give a name. Just a nod. And when he turned to accept his lot receipt, no one pressed him. Only Josh watched, jaw tight, as the man tucked his bidder card into his pocket and slipped back into the crowd like smoke.

Emily shifted her feet, a flicker of unease curling in her chest. Her eyes scanned the room, searching for Jared—but he was gone. And so was Josh.

A ripple of murmurs moved through the audience as the house lights dimmed, cloaking the room in an expectant hush.

Whatever had drawn them away, it was too late to follow.

Lot 5: The Hound of Blackwood Vale

Cast in bronze and modeled after Victor Barrow's eponymous hellhound. A physical manifestation commissioned by the late Florence Barrow to celebrate her husband's first publication. Once an icon of myth, now revealed as legend.

A single spotlight lit the stage behind Emily, the set portraying a blend of shadowy, sculpted trees and twisted branches that created the illusion of a moonlit forest. A faint mist hugged the floor, backlit with midnight blue lighting, to lend an ethereal glow.

Gareth glanced at Emily, who replied with a small nod.

The crowd leaned in, breath held, as projected shadows stretched and twisted across the backdrop—branches clawing at the darkness like skeletal fingers.

Then something *moved*.

Not the projection.

Something real.

A pair of red eyes flared to life in the darkness.

Gasps rippled through the audience as a single spotlight snapped on, slicing through the gloom to reveal Lucy.

She stood statue-still, ears pricked like horned silhouettes, the sharp white of her teeth catching the light as she panted—slow and rhythmic. The air seemed to thicken, pressing in, as if the room itself were holding its breath.

Then she moved.

Not like a trained canine, but like something summoned. Her paws glided across the timber stage with soundless precision, muscles coiled beneath her sleek coat. Behind her, a shadow stretched—twice her size, wrong in its proportions. The legs were too long. The spine too curved. And it didn't move with her. It lagged, then jolted to catch up.

Emily's throat tightened. The hair on her arms stood on end. She turned instinctively toward Jared to find he was back—watching her as if he'd never left. He frowned, eyes narrowed, like he was trying to make sense of it, too.

This wasn't theatrics.

This was something else. Something *other*.

Onstage, Lucy stopped at the edge. Her breath came faster now, vapor blooming in the beam of light despite the warmth of the room. Her eyes locked onto a point in the crowd—unblinking, intent. Then, with a low growl that rolled through the silence like distant thunder, she sprang.

The spotlight burst into darkness.

A collective gasp rang out as she vanished—into the blackness beneath the stage, and into the waiting hands of Josh.

And then Gareth's voice cut cleanly through the dark, steady and sure, but almost reverent now:

"This is the spectral beast that shaped a legend."

When the stage lights came back up, the backdrop lifted, revealing the statue.

Under the glare of an ultraviolet spotlight, its gleaming surface pulsed with menace in the dim glow of the room like something watching. Waiting.

The silence deepened.

Gareth picked up his gavel. "Opening at twenty."

Pendleton's paddle went up.

"Twenty thousand—do I hear twenty-two? Twenty-five! Thirty thousand dollars..."

Bidding erupted in a cacophony of raised paddles and escalating numbers. The atmosphere turned frenzied and the Pendleton representative, flushed and well out of his depth, lowered his paddle.

Gasps followed each raise, the audience hanging on every bid.

"Thirty-three."

A nod from the back.

"Thirty-five thousand dollars—sold!"

The gavel slammed down. The hall exploded with speculation.

Eyes turned toward Pendleton's side, defeat and anger sitting heavily on their shoulders.

Gareth, though composed, exuded an almost imperceptible relief as the auction reached its conclusion. "And so," he declared, "we bid farewell to a piece of literary history."

The audience, still murmuring with awe and excitement, rose from their seats. Pendleton's representatives were the first to leave. Jess was nowhere to be seen.

At the back of the room, Simon Reed stood with his arms crossed, a faint smile tugging at his mouth—small, and hovering somewhere between sorrow and satisfaction. Briony stood by his side.

His story was finally out. And for the first time in a week, Emily thought he looked lighter.

She, too, should have felt relief. Maybe even triumph. Instead, there was something else settling in her chest. Not an end. Not even closure. But something unfinished.

She looked for Jared and found him at the edge of the room, his eyes already on her. His tie was slightly askew again, as if he'd been pulling at his collar. He hadn't moved during the final lot. He'd simply watched her—steady and proud, like she was the most important thing in the room. But before she could celebrate the night's revelations, there was one last thing to face.

"I just need a minute," she mouthed, and Jared nodded without hesitation, understanding in his eyes.

Emily slipped away from the main room, weaving through the emptied gallery floor.

The Hound stood exactly like it had all evening. Still. Waiting. But no longer vigilant. She felt the shift immediately.

Before tonight, the statue's presence had been overwhelming—there was too much noise, too many threads tangled together. The fragmented details, the myths, the uncertainty—they clouded everything, kept her from truly grasping the weight of Barrow's last words. But now, with the truth spoken aloud, with Reed's speech setting Barrow free, there was no longer chaos. In the wake of everything laid bare, there was nothing left to obscure.

There was only clarity.

Emily reached out, pressing her palm gently atop the Hound's head. And the moment she connected with it, she saw him. Victor Barrow. At his desk, Montblanc in hand, head bent over his notebook.

Her vision focused on the page, and the last missing piece surfaced.

You always said a good editor sees between the lines, Frank. So read what's not written. You were right about Blackwood Vale. I've lost the line between story and memory, and I don't know what parts are still mine. But you always pulled me back. You always saw through the fog.

I'm sorry I left the weight of it on your shoulders. The publishers, the pressure—it was never about the books. It was the ghosts behind them. I know that now, yet I should've said it sooner.

If there's anything left worth saving, it's because of you. It's all for you.

Tell them the story. Tell them—

Emily closed her eyes for a moment, feeling the finality of it settle deep. The confirmation that Barrow's unfinished sentence wasn't an absence.

But a permission.

She drew in a slow, steadying breath. She *had* told them.

And now, she could step fully into what came next.

She turned away, moving back toward the room, toward Jared. He met her just offstage, hand outstretched.

He didn't speak as he helped her down the narrow steps, his grip steady, grounding. Her heels clicked softly against the wooden treads, a sound that felt louder than it was. When she reached the floor, he didn't let go.

"You did it," he murmured, his voice for her alone. "Now they know."

Emily met his gaze. "So do I."

For a moment, they simply stood there in the quiet aftermath, solid in the wake of truth. The air between them thrummed—not with urgency, but with confirmation.

Jared's hand found the small of her back, guiding her closer. She rested her head against his chest, eyes closed, breathing in the steadiness of him.

And when Jared raised her chin to look directly into his eyes, Emily knew—

They weren't standing in the aftermath.

They were standing at the beginning.

Epilogue

Loyalty and Legacy

A month later

The auction house was quiet.

Not silent—it was never quite that—there was always some collection being cataloged, some whisper of provenance to trace; but the fever of Victor Barrow's exhibit had passed. The drama had burned through the building like sunlight through fog, leaving behind a golden afterglow—warm, lingering, and full of possibility.

Emily walked the familiar halls to Jared's office, where she found him sitting behind his desk, brows drawn in familiar consternation.

She tapped gently on the open door.

His head lifted, and in the space of a heartbeat, his entire expression softened. The frown eased. The tension in his jaw released. What replaced it wasn't quite a smile—more of an unguarded warmth that lit his features from within. His eyes found hers and held. Drank her in. Like he'd been waiting for this moment all day.

"Hey," she said. "Are you ready for dinner?"

"Not really." He scrubbed a hand down his face. "Are you sure you want to do this? It's not too late to pull out, you know."

"And miss meeting the infamous Hunter Finch?"

"He's not all he's cracked up to be. Trust me."

"Your mom would never forgive us." She sauntered across the room and perched on the edge of his desk beside him. "What's going on?"

"Pendleton has challenged legitimacy of the data and launched a defamation campaign against both Simon Reed and us. Jess tells me it's a litigation nightmare, but they haven't got a leg to stand on."

"They're just scrambling. Trying to save face. We knew this would happen." She shifted closer to him on the desk. "Anyway, I have some news that might make you feel better."

His gaze dropped to the hem of her pencil skirt, now riding mid-thigh. "I think I'm already feeling better," he murmured.

She swatted his hand away from her leg. "Simon Reed's new publisher announced the biography this morning. It's due for release early next year."

Jared let out a low whistle. "That's going to send shockwaves through the industry." He raised his eyes to hers with an amused smile. "And we thought we ruffled feathers. What about the sixth Blackwood book?"

"He's launched an injunction to reclaim his rights under intellectual property, and with Pendleton undergoing a full corporate restructure, that should be cleared in a few months.

I've already pre-ordered copies for your bookshelf."

Jared's grin got wider. "See, there you go again. Always one step ahead."

Emily arched a brow. "Well, someone has to keep you on track."

"Then I hope this means I've caught up." He handed her a sheet of paper. "Have a read of this."

She took the sheet from him, his warm palm caressing her bare knee as she read the old-fashioned typewritten letter.

Dear Mr. Bell,

I hope this message finds you well. I wanted to apologize personally for trespassing on your property last week. I understand now how it must have looked, and I deeply regret not coming forward sooner.

Attached is the receipt for the lot I successfully bid on—Victor Barrow's typewriter. I know how strange this might sound, but I had to see it for myself. I grew up hearing stories from my grandfather about the "code games" he and my great-uncle Franklin used to play—replacing typebars, adjusting key levels to form subtle messages with the rise and fall of inked letters.

When I heard Victor Barrow's estate was being

opened, something clicked. My dad told me Frank was always telling him that a good editor knows how to read between the lines. I now know he was trying to tell him something—something hidden. I just didn't know how deep it went until I saw the original manuscripts at your auction.

Jessica Cotillard is working with me and helped me understand how to take the next step. I'm ready to stand up for what's right. For Great-Uncle Frank. And for Victor.

Thank you for handling the sale with such care. I know I shouldn't have gone behind your back—but I hope, in time, you'll understand why I had to.

Kind regards,
Ethan Graves

"That was him at the auction, wasn't it?" she whispered, thinking back to the bidder with the scripted ink flowing down their forearms. "Ethan."

"Josh clocked him going in, but since he'd registered and we hadn't pressed charges, there was nothing he could do."

"So, he was never after the Hound at all... He was only trying to gain access to Barrow's typewriter," Emily mused. "I wonder if Mia knew. Was she with him at the auction? I didn't see her."

"No. She never showed." He shook his head. "Probably a

good thing. Josh would've sent her packing."

"Hmm." Emily still felt sorry for the girl.

"Speaking of clandestine doings... Did Reed tell you about this?" He turned his laptop to face her and clicked on an email forwarded by Jess. It was a deed of gift, formalizing the transfer of ownership of the Hound statue without payment. The donor's identity had been redacted.

The recipient was Briony Reed.

Emily turned to Jared, eyes wide.

"Wait. It gets better." He opened an attachment. A photo of the Hound appeared on the screen, standing atop a pedestal not unlike the one in the Channings' garden. Only this one was indoors. Jared zoomed in on the brass plaque affixed beneath it.

The Hound of Blackwood Vale, circa 1978.
Donated to the National Library. On Permanent
Display.

"It's the centerpiece of an installation celebrating Barrow's contribution to Australian horror fiction."

"Wow. Looks like Simon and his daughter have given the old dog a second chance."

Jared stared at her. "I think a few of us have gotten those," he said quietly.

Sofia buzzed through on his desk phone to let him know that James and Margot were on their way in.

Jared barely had time to remove his hand from Emily's leg when Margot breezed through the door with her signature perfect style and thinly veiled scrutiny.

"How was London?" Emily asked, drawing to her feet.

"Tiring," James answered with a yawn. "And cold. Always cold."

Margot shot her husband a look. "While your father slept like a baby on the flight home, I went over the auction accounts, and... you did well," Margot said, surprising Emily by rounding the desk and laying a soft hand on her elbow. "Seems it was rather effective, after all."

"Dramatic, for sure," James added. "But justice isn't always silent. Sometimes it needs a stage."

Emily met his eyes and nodded. "Sometimes it does."

"Anyway, we just wanted to give you the congratulations in person before dinner. Are you both ready?" Margot eyed her son suspiciously.

Jared rolled his eyes good-naturedly. "You two head on over. We just have a couple of things to tie up here first."

"Good lad," James muttered, ushering Margot out with a hand on the small of her back. He threw a wink over his shoulder at Emily, who smiled at the gesture.

When they were gone, Jared let out a low breath and nudged her shoulder. "That was their way of saying they approve, you know."

Emily looked up at him, lips quirking. "You think?"

"Trust me. That was a standing ovation."

She laughed softly, the energy between them humming in the quiet of his office. With a teasing glance, she smoothed the fabric of her skirt. "Come on. If we don't get moving, your mom will assume I've been leading you astray."

Jared chuckled, grabbing her around the waist. "I'd tell her she's not far off."

She broke away from him reluctantly and ducked into her own office to grab her purse. Slinging it over her shoulder, she skipped down the stairs and together they stepped out into the late summer evening. The fading sunlight reflected off the multi-paned windows of the neighboring buildings, turning the entire street golden, and Emily took a moment to glance back at the heritage building she now called home—at least for the moment.

She hadn't had much luck finding her own place since arriving in Sydney, and Jared didn't seem in any hurry to kick her out of his loft. Not that she was complaining.

He slipped an arm around her shoulders as they walked, pulling her in close. His mouth brushed her ear, the graze of his stubble raising goosebumps along her neck. "I can't wait to kiss that lipstick off your mouth."

"Is it too much?" She smirked. "I was thinking of switching to a less dangerous shade."

"Don't you dare."

Grinning, she reached into her clutch for a mint—then froze as her fingers wrapped around something that didn't belong there.

A powder compact.

It was silver, tarnished at the edges, the curved lid finely embossed with a delicate decorative pattern. Old. Expensive. A piece with history.

She frowned, thumb brushing its surface. "This isn't mine."

Jared, who was letting his mom know they were on their way, paused mid-text. "Where did that come from?"

"I've no idea." She turned it over in her hand. The lid clicked open, and Emily's step faltered.

The mirror inside was shattered.

But just for a second, in the dying rays of the sun, Emily was certain she saw a face in the shards.

Only the reflection wasn't hers.

It belonged to someone else.

Someone long gone—if the cold bleeding up her arm was any sign.

Quickly, she snapped it closed before the pavement tilted beneath her feet.

She looked to Jared, heart ticking faster. "But it looks like we've got another story to chase."

He grinned, slipping his arm around her waist. "I was hoping you'd say that."

Want to know how it all began?

Dive into the origins of *Deadly Possessions* with the FREE prequel! Uncover the secrets, meet the characters before their destinies unfold, and experience the beginning of everything. Download ***A Bird in the Hand*** now and start the adventure!

https://BookHip.com/CJHWRMS

Don't miss the chilling start of *Reflecting on Death*, Book 2 in the *Deadly Possessions* series.

Turn the page for a preview!

Reflecting on Death

In **_Reflecting on Death_**, psychic researcher Emily Sloane and her auctioneer partner Jared Bell return for another haunting mystery—this time, linked to an opulent art déco compact and the double life of its former owner, Clara Everleigh, a spiritualist's assistant and vaudeville performer in 1920s Melbourne.

When a powerful vision unlocks Clara's final moments—a darkened rooftop, a glittering party, and a sudden fall—Emily knows her death wasn't an accident. But as her clairtangent abilities intensify, so do the risks, drawing her and Jared into the shadowy past of the newly restored Hotel Carillon, where ambition, betrayal, and forbidden love once collided.

As they untangle a story silenced for nearly a century, a new danger emerges in the present day—someone will do anything to keep Clara's secrets buried. And when the past begins bleeding into the present, Emily must decide how far she's willing to go to give the dead a voice.

Because some mirrors don't just reflect the past—they demand justice.

I

Reflections and Reservations

The restaurant perched above the city like a glass jewel box, glittering against the deep blue twilight. Emily tightened her grip on her purse as Jared guided her through the maze of marble-topped tables. Even with his warm fingers threaded through hers, a cold dread snaked through her, a certainty that she was carrying something forbidden, something that felt heavy and wrong.

She smoothed a hand down her skirt as Jared stopped before a table tucked alongside the glass balcony railing. James and Margot Bell were already seated, champagne on ice between them, their smiles bright and faintly expectant. The table was set for six.

"So glad you decided to finally join us," Margot said, with a pointed look at her son.

"Didn't you get my message?" Jared asked, as he pulled out a chair for Emily, seating himself beside her. He pointed to the empty place setting across from him, adding sarcastically, "I see Hunter is his usual punctual self, yet I don't hear you criticizing him."

"He let us know he'd be late," Margot replied.

"I sent you a text letting you know we were on our way," Jared said defensively, pulling out his phone. "Didn't you get it?"

Emily watched as he glanced at the screen, cursed under his breath and quietly deleted the unfinished text to his mom. He hadn't sent it—her discovery of the compact must have distracted him. She gave his knee a quick reassuring squeeze under the table.

"So, Emily—how is Sydney treating you? Have you seen much of our fair city yet?" James asked, just as Jared reached under the table and placed his hand over hers, anchoring it against his thigh.

Distracted, she turned to his father with a smile.

"It's been a bit of a whirlwind, to be honest," she said, "but I thrive on the chaos. One thing's for certain, I could definitely get used to Monday night dinners like this."

"I thought you liked my cooking!" Jared exclaimed with mock outrage.

She laughed. "You know I do. I just don't think we've had a Monday dinner at home since I got here."

Emily didn't miss the subtle quirk of Margot's brow at her use of the word "home" but Jared was already teasing about how they could switch back to burgers and Monday night football if she preferred.

Clearly not ready to let the moment slide, Margot sipped her champagne and asked how the apartment hunting was going.

"Not well," Emily admitted. "Everything gets snapped up in a heartbeat. I haven't even been able to get in any inspections."

James sighed. "The market can be brutal. Especially if you don't have a local rental history. You either need a miracle... or an inside connection."

The latter was said with a sly smile that implied something Emily didn't quite follow.

But Jared caught on immediately. "Not a chance, Dad."

"Oh, come on," James said with a laugh. "I'm sure he'd be open to the idea. You just need to stop being so stubborn."

Jared shook his head and knocked back his champagne like water.

Emily looked to Margot for guidance. "What are they talking about?"

"Speak of the devil," Jared announced, standing.

"In the flesh," said a voice with the kind of British crispness that was dry, deliberate, and entirely too self-possessed.

She glanced past Jared to find a man dressed in a black button-down and tailored slacks approaching their table. He stopped and pulled Jared into a brotherly hug before turning his attention to her.

Hunter Finch.

His features were striking in a way that mirrored Jared's, only darker—sharper. Where Jared's warmth felt lived-in, Hunter's charisma was honed, commanding in a way that drew attention even when he wasn't trying.

He offered her his hand and a polite but curious smile. "And you must be the delightful Emily. I was beginning to think Jay made you up."

Emily smiled and accepted his handshake. "Nice to meet you."

"Likewise." His gaze held hers for a second longer than necessary—not intrusive, but measured—before he rounded the table, pressing a kiss to Margot's cheek and clapping James on the shoulder. "Talking about me again? Must be a slow news night."

James set down his glass with an easy grin. "Emily's been apartment hunting."

"I've been trying, yes. Sydney isn't exactly renter-friendly."

Hunter slid into the empty seat across from her, pouring himself a glass of champagne.

"Depends on who you know. I might be able to help you out. Has Jay shown you The Argyle Residences at Millers Point?"

Emily shook her head. "No, I haven't been out much lately—but the name sounds familiar."

"We've just finished restoring a heritage site there. Original architecture, modern interiors, loads of character. It's the kind of place that doesn't open to just anyone. You have to be in the know." He glanced over at Jared, then back at her. "And you have the right connections. Although I honestly don't blame my brother for wanting to keep you all to himself. But if you want your own space close enough to Bell's without living on top of it, you should swing by. Take a look."

Jared dipped his head close to her ear, his breath warm against her cheek. "Indulge him and agree, otherwise he won't shut up about it all night. He gets off on sales pitches."

Emily offered a diplomatic smile. "That's very generous of you, Hunter. I'll keep it in mind."

Hunter raised his glass slightly in her direction. "No pressure. Just an invitation."

"Is that why you're here—to oversee the development?"

"Partly," Hunter said, settling back into his chair with that same easy poise she'd come to recognize in Jared. "And partly for this." He lifted his champagne flute toward the table. "Family bonding. Bubbles. Drama, if we're lucky."

Jared gave a wry smile. "It wouldn't be a visit from you without it."

"Guilty. Though I imagine things might get more interesting after dinner." Hunter's grin sharpened. "I invited Jess to swing by for a drink."

Emily felt Jared stiffen beside her, though his voice remained level. "Did you now?"

"She's in the neighborhood. Thought I'd say hello. Figured you wouldn't mind."

"Not at all," Jared said coolly. "Just wondering what you're angling for."

"Who says I'm angling?" Hunter raised his glass to his lips, the picture of innocence.

Margot cleared her throat and flicked open her menu. "Unless one of you is literally catching fish, I suggest we choose something to eat."

Emily offered Jared a soft smile, then picked up her menu—but the words blurred behind a fog of rising tension. Jess. Of course Jess. She hadn't expected to feel so thrown by the mention of Jared's ex but the brothers' veiled animosity and the tightening in her chest said otherwise.

She lowered her menu. "Order me something with chicken?" she said to Jared quietly. "I just need to..." She gestured vaguely toward the back of the restaurant. "Freshen up."

He glanced at her, concern flickering behind his eyes. "You okay?"

"Fine," she said, a little too brightly. "The champagne's just nudging a headache."

Before he could question it, she slipped from her chair and all but fled toward the restrooms. She needed space—away from the mention of Jess, from whatever game Hunter was playing, and from the feeling that she was once again an outsider, peering through the glass at a life that would never be hers.

And throughout it all, the compact had been whispering at the edges of her thoughts, humming with a secret she couldn't unravel yet. Perhaps a moment alone with it might just be the distraction she needed.

She barely heard the soft click of the powder room door behind her as she slipped inside, her pulse drumming hollowly in her ears. The dark tiles and subdued lighting were an instant relief, easing the sudden ache behind her eyes. It seemed a real headache was developing, after all.

She went to the basin and wet her hands, before pressing

them to the back of her neck. A cold trickle of water descended across the front of her throat and she watched it in the mirror, pondering what events the smoky glass had witnessed in its brief existence.

Clearly nothing as tragic as the one in her purse.

Reaching into her clutch, she drew out the compact and studied the design on the lid—a delicate pattern of interwoven floral vines. Vintage art déco, likely late 1920s or early '30s. The back wasn't metal, oddly. Instead, it was covered in a coarse ditsy print fabric, its weave just rough enough to catch a fingernail. A shallow indent along the rim suggested the fabric had once been covered with metallic mesh—now long gone. She'd seen similar designs in college while studying Art Nouveau, but never one quite like this.

It was beautiful, certainly. But also... *off*.

As her fingers brushed the fabric again, a faint chill prickled her skin—not from the compact itself, but from the echo of what was missing. It was as if the ghost of that cold mesh still lingered, resting against her palm.

Flicking the clasp, she opened the lid, careful not to catch her reflection in the broken glass. Inside, the powder pan held only the faintest traces of product, the pale pink puff still surprisingly soft despite its age.

"What a beautiful piece. A new estate find?" Margot's voice rang out sharp against the hush of the bathroom.

Emily startled—she hadn't heard her come in. For a brief second she considered lying about the compact's provenance but Jared's once-made point—that his mother could spot a fake from across the harbor—rang loud and clear in her memory.

Settling on a version of the truth, she shook her head.

"No, actually. I just found it. I must have picked up the wrong clutch at that industry mixer on Friday night."

Margot's keen gaze dropped to Emily's handbag—a black satin Carolina Herrera cigar-box style clutch, complete with its signature jade clasp. A twenty-first birthday gift from her best friend, Isobel.

Emily let out a slow breath. It was unlikely that someone at the mixer had the same purse as hers, but not impossible. Plausible enough to satisfy Margot, at least.

Still, it didn't explain the fractured mirror.

"May I?" Margot held out an elegant hand.

Emily passed the compact over with fingers that felt suddenly unsteady.

Margot pulled a tiny loupe from the chain at her neck and peered closely at the compact's interior.

"It could be an Evans," she murmured. "There's no hallmark, but not all of them were marked. Shame about the mirror. Did you drop it?"

"No. It was already like that when I opened it just now. Do you think that's what happened? It was dropped?"

Margot turned the compact under the light. "See here? That's an impact fissure."

She handed Emily the loupe. Despite her earlier reluctance, Emily leaned forward, the instinct to understand overtaking her unease.

The point of impact lay just above the hinge, where a tight cluster of fractures bloomed, delicate as a spiderweb but jagged enough to catch the light and split her face right down the middle.

A pretty young woman stared back at her from the right hand side—light brown curls, one heavily kohled green eye and ruby-red lips parted in a silent scream.

And then... she *moved*.

Not Emily. But the *other* half of her reflection.

The half-girl vanished off the edge of the glass. Reappeared. Screamed. Vanished again. The motion played out in a grotesque loop, like an old film caught on repeat.

Emily snapped the compact shut with a click and staggered backward, the floor suddenly falling away beneath her. She clutched at the basin to stop from falling. Margot's loupe slipped from her hand, clattering into the sink as Emily's vision distorted to a gaping black void surrounded by jagged rainbow shards.

A migraine aura. One of the worst she'd ever had.

Her painkillers were back at Jared's place, tucked in the drawer of the ensuite she'd slowly started thinking of as hers.

"Emily?" Margot's voice was sharp now. "Are you feeling ill?"

Emily tried to shake her head, but the motion only worsened the pain. She pressed a hand to her forehead. It felt as though a knife was being driven down through her skull behind her right eye.

No. Not a cluster. Not now.

"I'll fetch Jared."

Margot swept out just as the bathroom door opened, letting in three laughing young women and the lively clink of glassware and bright jazz from the restaurant.

"Girl, are you all right?" one of the women asked.

"Migraine," Emily gritted out.

"Oh honey, I've got Mersyndol," said another, rifling through her purse. She pulled out a blue-and-white box and pressed it into Emily's hand. "Take it."

Emily blinked at the woman, but couldn't see her face, let alone what was printed on the blister packet. She could have been giving her mollie for all she knew.

Didn't matter. She'd take anything to dull the stabbing sensation in her head.

"Thanks." She popped two of the yellow pills and drank straight from the faucet.

The women vanished into the stalls. Then the door opened again.

A woman approached her from behind, but in the bathroom mirror, her features were swallowed entirely by the spreading aura.

"Jesus, Em."

Jess.

Her voice was tinged with something close to genuine concern. "You look like you've seen a ghost."

A Note for the Curious Reader

Feel like solving a mystery right alongside Emily?

Each book in the *Deadly Possessions* series hides its own secret page — a little tucked-away corner of my website where a clue is waiting just for you. Collect the phrase for this book, gather all six across the series, and you'll earn a special reward made for the truly curious.

Your next clue is ready whenever you are.
Follow the link below (or scan the QR code) and step into the fun.

Welcome to The Curiosity Club.

About the Author

Melanie Pickering writes urban gothic thrillers and dark cozy mysteries shaped by atmosphere, history, and the quiet details that linger in old things and even older places.

Find her online:
melaniepickering.com | @melaniepickeringwrites

Join her Facebook Readers Group:
https://www.facebook.com/groups/melaniesdeadlypossessions